FLICKERS

FLICKERS

Arthur Slade

HarperCollins*PublishersLtd*

For Tanaya

FLICKERS

1913
Near Lethbridge, Alberta

The first baby was born after midnight on the kitchen table of a two-room ranch house. It was December 16. A massive snowstorm shrouded the countryside. The old rancher, Ernest Thorn, had to perform the delivery as there was no way to plough through twenty miles of swirling snow and drifts to Lethbridge. He wasn't even certain he could open his front door, the snowbanks had piled so high. Hot water boiled on the pot-bellied stove and warm blankets waited on the cupboard next to the table. He washed his hands with whisky.

"It's time," his wife said through clenched teeth.

The rancher wasn't surprised by Abigail's bravery and strength; she had been strong enough to live in a sod house next to the Oldman River for eight years before he built this two-bedroom log house. She had done every chore this ranching life demanded of her without complaint. "Just push," he said, patting her hand. "Nature will do the rest."

As the snow drifted deeper around the house and the wind rattled the glass in the windows, Ernest guided his daughter into the world. It was a surprisingly quick and easy birth. She was smaller than he'd expected. He held the gently crying infant in his crooked, callused hands and looked into her eyes, the same blue as his wife's.

He was a hard man. He'd fought in the Boer War, had fought drought and pestilence and time, and it was rare that he was ever moved by beauty, but in the infant's soft, small features he saw angelic perfection.

"Is she . . . healthy?" his wife asked, her voice drowsy with exhaustion.

"Yes. Yes." He wrapped the girl in linen. "She's gloriously well formed."

He laid the squirming bundle in his wife's outstretched arms. "She's exquisite," Abigail rasped, after catching her breath. "She's a gift from God."

"What will we call her?" Ernest asked.

"Isabelle," his wife answered without hesitation. It had been her mother's name and it suited the baby. She was destined to be a belle of the prairies.

Ernest wondered how he had deserved to have such grace in his life. Not once, but twice. The first time was ten years ago when his wife had chosen him, in spite of his being much older than her and even though so many other men had asked for her hand in marriage. And now, here was an angel wriggling before them. After such a long wait there would be three Thorns to till the soil. And maybe even a boy next. He patted his wife's hand again and smiled.

She opened her mouth to speak but instead screamed a hard and terrible scream.

Ernest quickly laid Isabelle in the waiting bassinet. His daughter mewled and reached for him, her cries hitting a higher and higher pitch, but he left her there.

"What's happening?" he asked Abigail. "What's wrong?"

"Another ch-child," she said. "There's another child. A twin." Then Abigail screamed again, the tendons on her neck standing out. She gritted her teeth, grabbed the edges of the table and breathed madly, like a horse with a broken leg. "Dear God," she said.

The crown of the infant was showing. Ernest had pulled hundreds of calves into this world and he knew the baby would suffocate if he delayed a moment longer. So he helped in his own rough way, sweat forming on his forehead. Then, with one more short scream from his wife, the infant was free and squirming in his hands.

The rancher held it up: another daughter, heavier than the first and more solid. Her skin was a patchwork of purple and white, the umbilical cord tight around her neck. He loosened the cord and she began sucking in wet breaths. She made no other noise, just looked up at him with eyes as brown as his own.

The girl was so unlike her sister that it shocked him. He had seen calves born hairless, their skin a human pink, their goggling eyes odd and far too large. She was as wretched as those calves, her skull misshapen, perhaps by the force he'd applied when he'd pulled her. Her naked body was covered with brown spots—dozens of birthmarks on her arms, legs, chest, and face.

"It's—it's another daughter." Then, a moment later, he added, "Abigail?"

His wife was still. Her chest did not rise. He knew in his gut she was dead. Her heart had given out bringing their second daughter into the world.

The twin didn't look as though she belonged here. It was as if he'd wrenched her from some other place.

2

The news of the twins' birth and Abigail Thorn's death travelled quickly up the Oldman River to Lethbridge and farther along the rail line to Calgary and down to Sweetgrass, Montana. People in the southwest section of the province knew the old rancher; he'd been one of the first in those parts to leave the coal mines and successfully carve a farm into the hilly land.

The doctor came and pronounced the children healthy, but warned that the birthmarks on the younger girl's skin would never go away. Isabelle had cried for a long time after the doctor left. Ernest offered her more milk and changed her dry diaper, but to no avail. He decided she was a social child. She'd gotten that from her mother.

A reporter from the *Lethbridge Herald* arrived, but Ernest only allowed him to photograph Isabelle. No sense having strangers gawk at the ugly daughter. Her photograph was carried by several papers and the sight of her, and the story of her birth, touched thousands of hearts. Within a week, Ernest had received several packages of infant clothing and more baby food and formula than twenty children would consume in a lifetime. This was followed by bundles of blankets sent by church groups, letters from men saying they were available to work his fields for free, women offering to clean and cook, and even a proposal of marriage from an ancient widow in Calgary. At least thirty people wired money. And one old sailor from the East Coast sent a box of dried fish. Ernest took one whiff of it and fed the fish to the barn cats. He silently thanked the fisherman and all the other kind strangers.

Neighbours offered to care for his children, but he refused—the girls were all he had left of Abigail. So he learned to feed them Mellin's Infant Food and milk from his Jersey cow. He boiled their dirty diapers and folded them in neat piles.

Two weeks after their births, Ernest realized he had yet to name the younger sister. He was avoiding it—almost as if he didn't want to claim her as his own. It was time, though.

He brought Isabelle out of the bedroom and set her in the bassinet near the fire. She began to cry the moment he walked away. Then he retrieved her sister. Once they were side by side Isabelle calmed down. The younger girl had one arm on Isabelle, but watched him with such serious eyes. Or so it appeared; he wasn't certain how much children could see this early in life.

"Beatrice," he said. The name seemed to have come out of nowhere. It took him a moment to remember that Beatrice was a character in one of the fancy poetry books Abigail had been reading. She'd babble constantly about poetry and book stories over dinner.

Beatrice. Abigail would approve.

In February, the snow deepened and the storms became so terrible that he tied a long rope from the barn to his house. Hand over hand he went, the whiteness so blinding that if he took one step off the path, he could easily stumble into a field and freeze to death before he found his way back. To his surprise, both the children thrived during the hard winter. Isabelle began to make more and more gurgles, and he was certain that her speech would come easily and early. He played peekaboo and upsy-daisy with her. But if he went away or picked up Beatrice, she shrieked.

So he would wait until Isabelle slept to take Beatrice into his arms. When he lifted her into a sitting position, she'd hold her head straight. She was strong and was already rolling over. Maybe she'd be like a son.

He tried to find beauty in Beatrice's face, but it was too lopsided and the skin hadn't decided which colour it wanted to be. Some parts were dark pink, others marred by the birthmarks. It made her look a bit like a calico cat. The marks seemed to form a pattern, but he couldn't make sense of it. Though Isabelle already had her first strands of blond hair, it seemed Beatrice's hair might never grow. It didn't matter. There were hats. And he would protect her from any who were gruff enough or stupid enough to remark about her appearance within his earshot.

He began to believe there would be something good for his children in the future. He'd fight this hard world for it and carve a place for them, and they would have happy lives.

3

1914
Near Lethbridge, Alberta

With the spring thaw, icicles began to drip and the snow melted to reveal brown earth and dead grass. Ernest was in the front yard chopping wood for the stove, both girls asleep in the house, when he heard a rumbling. He turned, axe in hand, to see a black automobile snaking along the road. It was the largest car Ernest had ever seen. The driver sat in an open-air compartment, goggles guarding his eyes and around his neck was a red muffler that flapped like a flag. His purple coat and leather hat made him look like a pilot. In the seat next to him sat a blond woman in a green coat. The windows of the carriage section were dark.

The car stopped at the edge of the driveway, one front wheel on the grass. The driver stepped out, lifted his goggles, and smiled, showing perfectly white teeth. He opened the door on the passenger side and made a show of taking the woman's hand and helping her step down. It was as if they were acting in a play; they turned in unison and walked arm in arm toward Ernest, the woman's open coat flapping in the wind. In his opinion, too many buttons were undone at the top of her dress. She stumbled on a rut, straightened herself, and let out a girlish giggle.

"Uncle Ernest," the driver said.

Ernest squinted, then recognized his nephew. He hadn't seen his sister's son in several years. The boy was now in his late twenties, his dark hair was combed straight back with oil, except for one curiously silver lock that curled across his brow. The woman was attractive and maybe twenty, cheeks red with the wind, eyes a little red, too, and her smile strained. She giggled again.

"Wayne," Ernest said. He put no warmth in his reply. He had labelled his nephew a drifter when the boy was a teen and Wayne had proved him right by drifting away from his family farm, his responsibilities. He hadn't even come home for his mother's funeral. "You've aged."

"Grown up, you mean. I've been working in California. In the flicker show industry down there. Have you ever seen one?"

"I don't have time for flights of fancy."

Wayne laughed. "I suppose you don't. Cows to feed and fields to till. My work is much different now. I've been in some brilliant films. I was in *Trail to the West* and *The Deserter* and had bit parts in several others. Betty is in movies, too." She curtsied a little too deeply and Wayne caught her before she toppled over. "She's going to be a big star."

That got her laughing again, a sound that set Ernest's teeth on edge. *She's drunk*, he thought. The red eyes. The giggles. *The woman is drunk!*

"Why are you here?" Ernest asked. He hadn't lowered the axe yet.

"You always were quick to the point, Uncle. That's what I like about you." Wayne put his hat back on at the perfect angle. "Well, I saw the picture."

"Picture?"

"Yes, of your daughter. Of Isabelle Thorn. Aunt Jessop clipped it from the Lethbridge paper and mailed it my way. It's made quite the buzz down south. You didn't know that?"

"How would I?"

"Good question. Good question." He scratched his head as if pondering that very thing. "Well, when I saw the little baby I just knew I had to visit my brand-spanking-new cousin. Can we go inside?"

"We'd love to see the sweet little one," Betty said. "She must be cute in a dress. I brought one. A gift for her. It's very frilly."

"The girls are sleeping," Ernest said.

"Girls?" Wayne continued to scratch his head. "Oh, that's right, they're twins. Even better. That's a handful for an old rancher, isn't it? I mean, I know you can handle several cows. But kids, well, they're different animals altogether. All that crying and wailing and diapers and stuff."

"I get by."

"I suppose you do. But you know, Uncle Ernest, you can do much better than just getting by." He raised his eyebrows in a playful manner. "You'll be happy to hear that I've come with a wonderful proposition." He pointed at the car behind him. "You see, my boss—Mr. Big Picture Guy, as

I like to call him—he knows faces. He launched them all. Mary Pickford—he picked her out of a crowd of actresses. Douglas Fairbanks, too. Charlie Chaplin is a good friend of his. Like I say, Mr. Big Picture Guy has a sharp eye."

"Your boss not able to speak for himself?" Ernest asked.

Wayne laughed again. "He's the type who doesn't have to speak for himself."

"I don't let others wag their tongues for me. Does he have a name?"

"It's Mr. Cecil. He's a producer and a director—he's very well-known in important circles—the film industry, senators, oilmen. Anyway, he thought we could help you out."

"Help me? In what way?"

Wayne flashed another smile. "We'll raise them for you. Both of the girls. We have a lovely place, it's a mansion—one of the largest in the country, there're even tennis courts and a pool and a zoo and it's all right on the ocean. A California mansion. La Casa Grande. It has its own name, that's how big it is. Mr. Cecil is letting Betty and me live there. We're going to be his biggest stars. And that mansion is where your girls could grow up. A giant piece of heaven."

"You and this woman would raise them? Is she your wife?"

"Well, we got married on a film once. That counts, right? Truth is, we're fixin' to hitch real soon. She'd be a great mommy. Wouldn't you, Betty?"

"Of course. I like kids. Love 'em! I really do. They're so . . . so . . ."—she put her hands together as if she were holding one—". . . so little. They're like dolls. I love dolls."

Wayne added, "And there's no winter down there. None at all."

Ernest let out a snort. "You want them to live in a place with no winter?"

"Yes. Yes, of course. I know you have doubts, Uncle, but we've come all this way to make this extremely generous offer. You see, Isabelle has a wonderful face. Mr. Cecil sees great potential in it."

"What would he do with her face?"

"She would be in films! When she's older of course, though there are a few parts for babies and toddlers. Cute parts. It's a very lucrative business. After just a few years she could own a hundred farms like this."

"Why would I send my daughters so far away from where they were born?"

"Where we are born is not always the best place for us to end up." Wayne said each word slowly. "Dear Aunt Abigail would agree if she were still alive. All their education, all their needs would be looked after for the rest of their lives. They'd get everything they ever dreamed of. And Isabelle's name would be in lights."

Ernest glared at him.

Wayne glanced back at the vehicle. "Now, we're very reasonable, Uncle. We would pay you."

"Miss Betty," Ernest said, his voice gravelly, "would you trot on back to the car? I have words for my nephew's ears only."

Betty curtsied again. "His ears are all yours." She turned and wobbled away.

"You'd like to pay me for my children?" Ernest echoed.

"Money is no object. It could be a salary, if that's more to your liking. You could fix things up here—everything, that is. Buy another cow or two or ten."

With each word Ernest's hand was tightening on the axe handle. "My children can't be bought." It came out as a low growl. "Slither right back to your den of snakes."

"Now, now, Uncle Ernest. You're jumping to the wrong conclusion."

"No. Your mother is dead. Your father is dead. You're not my nephew. I'll have no further contact with you. Leave my farm."

Ernest Thorn stepped toward his nephew and Wayne backed up, raising his hands.

"Perhaps I worded things wrongly."

"No, you worded them the only way you know how. A lie. A twist. Another lie: whatever is best for you. Get out of here now if you want to leave in one piece." Wayne continued to back up. He glanced at the blacked-out windows of the car, then fled around the front, opened the driver's door, and threw himself into his seat.

Ernest stood ten feet away from the automobile, holding his axe. He wanted to attack the metal monster, to kill the thing that had brought them all here. He took a few steps toward the carriage compartment, staring into the blackened windows. "If you can hear me in there, Mr. Cecil, don't come back! This isn't California. This is my home. You're not welcome."

There was no reaction. Ernest could have been yelling into a cave, at a stone idol, or into the eye of a hurricane. The silence that followed brought an uneasy feeling to his guts.

"Get out of here!" he forced himself to shout. "They're my girls. Mine! Go! Get off my land."

Wayne nodded, though Ernest wasn't certain whether he was nodding to him or to a message somehow passed from the back compartment. His nephew fired up the motor of the car and slowly rolled ahead, then made a wide turn. He didn't look back. The car rumbled down the narrow road.

Ernest watched until they had disappeared into the horizon. Only then did he loosen his grip on the axe.

4

The following morning started out as had the past hundred mornings. Ernest awakened before sunrise, pulled on his clothes, threw two logs into the pot-bellied stove, put on his mud-caked boots at the door, and went out to milk the Jersey cow. His wife had named the cow Blackeye because of a rather ominous patch of black hide on one side of her face that accented the hard craziness in her eyes. The cow had never submitted meekly to the humility of being milked. Despite that, he had grown attached to her. She had more personality than most human beings he'd met.

It had been a good winter with Blackeye, though. She'd been more agreeable since the birth of the twins. Ernest wondered if the old bag of milk and bones was happier now that her milk was going to the young lives growing up inside the house.

"Beatrice can crawl like the devil now," he said as he opened the gate to the milking stall. "And Isabelle holds her head up straight and strong. All thanks to your milk."

Blackeye seemed to nod in agreement and went directly to her stall without trying to charge or kick him. He tied her halter to the post and she chewed contentedly on her hay as he drew the milk from her. *Shup shup shup,* went the milk into the pail. He fell into the hypnotic rhythm of milking her.

He'd left the barn door open and the light of the rising sun was coming in the doorway. It was rising earlier and earlier each day, melting the last few dirty snowbanks, getting the grass to grow. Soon he would be seeding his land and waiting for the soft green tendrils of wheat to poke toward the sky. Maybe this year it would be a good crop.

The slight buzzing of an insect interrupted his thoughts. At first he decided it was his imagination. It was too early in the spring for insects, and there had been a ringing between his ears ever since he stepped too close to a firing cannon in South Africa. He glimpsed a movement out of the corner of his eye, but before he could focus the insect was gone. It was certainly larger than a fly. A hornet? He'd never seen a hornet before the last of the snow was gone.

He continued to milk, again lost in the *shup shup shupping* sound. The buzzing returned and Blackeye flicked her tail and shivered her hide, the age-old method of getting rid of bothersome insects. She slapped her tail again. Ernest knew it would be safest to pull the pail out now, but her udder wasn't quite empty. No sense leaving that milk inside her.

Something dropped out of the air and landed on her hip, just out of Ernest's reach. The insect was not one he'd seen before. It was the size of his little finger with a somewhat serpentine body, hornet wings, and two large black eyes. What the hell was it?

The thing's long scorpion-like tail snapped into the air then stabbed down and stung the cow.

Blackeye let out a harsh bellow, lifted her massive left foot, and kicked, striking Ernest in the right forearm. He heard a snap and felt a lightning bolt of pain. Then came the clatter of the pail as the milk spilled over his legs and splattered the straw. He cursed and backed away from Blackeye, who was now kicking and snorting, eyes wide and wild. She pulled her rope tight, seeming strong enough to bring the whole barn down.

Ernest grimaced as he rolled back his sleeve to discover that his forearm was bent at an odd angle. There was a bit of bone sticking out, blood leaking from the hole. He'd seen these kinds of injuries enough times on the battlefield. A rush of memory came over him and he was thrust back into the war, unsteady on his feet, the Boer field guns tearing open the ground, rifle fire and smoke all around. He blinked and took a deep breath. The guns continued to fire, but he was still in the barn. It became clear that Blackeye was kicking again and again, breaking the boards behind her stall, which sounded like guns going off. She was going to choke herself on the rope. He squeezed up next to her, yanked with his left hand on the slip knot, and she crashed into the barn wall. She swung her head, sizing him up for a charge. *Why didn't I dehorn you?* he wondered. Then she turned and barrelled out of the barn and into the farmyard. He didn't know if the barbed-wire fence would be enough to stop her. She'd race all the way to Montana.

He examined his injury. He wouldn't be able to set his own arm, he knew that much—it was too horribly broken.

He took a deep breath and kicked hard at a nearby pitchfork, breaking the handle. He clenched his teeth and used the handle and a halter rope to brace his arm. It took all his will not to vomit from the pain.

Ernest stumbled out the barn door and up the path to the house, his head aching, his vision fading, then turning bright. He didn't want to pass out. Especially not here. It was still cold enough he'd freeze in a few hours.

There was no way to send a message to his nieghbours. How would he get himself and both girls to town to see the doctor? No, he couldn't have the townspeople staring at them. Not at his Beatrice. He trusted the Paulsens, who lived only three miles away. Good people. They could keep their mouths shut. He'd have to rig up the wagon, not an easy thing to do with one arm, and the horse hadn't pulled anything for at least a month. But Ernest was strong enough to do it all left-handed as long as he didn't collapse. He'd leave the girls with the Paulsens, then make his way to town.

He shoved at the door to the house and it jammed about two inches in. Smoke! Was the stove's chimney pipe blocked again? A buzzing. Three more of those foul insects shot out the crack in the door. He slapped at them, but only managed to throw himself off balance. Then he heard fearful crying— both of the girls were screaming. He slammed into the door, banging his injured arm. That nearly made him black out. But he gritted his teeth and shouldered his way in.

The stove door was wide open. How could that be? He never forgot to close it. Embers had spilled out onto the floor and the rug was on fire and flames were shooting up the moth-ridden curtains. The forge-hot heat made his forehead sweat.

Isabelle was screaming as if she recognized the danger. Beatrice coughed and shouted her own cries and coughed again. He charged toward his children, bending low to stay below the worst of the smoke. Several long strides later, he reached down to grab Isabelle, then tried to use his right hand to scoop up Beatrice but a shock of pain shot through it and his hand failed to close. She tumbled out onto the floor.

The flames licked at his pant legs, his shirt, devouring the house so much faster than he'd have thought possible, sucking all the air right out of his lungs. Isabelle let out a shriek and, as if that were a command, he turned and ran. He stumbled outside, gasping for breath and rushed right to the barn and gently lowered Isabelle into a pile of straw. When he turned back, he saw that the flames were already dancing across the roof of his home.

Beatrice! His heart thudded in his chest and his stomach was knotted tight. Had he chosen one over the other? He coughed so hard he worried a lung would come up. He hadn't left a single soldier behind in any of his missions. He wouldn't leave Beatrice. He charged back across the yard and into the house—into the mouth of hell—striding through smoke and cannon fire. Memories of the war became real: soldiers were dying beside him, horses falling over from bullet wounds, shells landing in the foreground. He ran by them all. There was more buzzing and he was certain that a swarm of those horrible insects was circling around him, making his ears ring even louder. Beatrice was on the floor where she had fallen, and he was thankful to see that the fire hadn't yet claimed her. She had wriggled out of the blanket, trying to crawl away.

"Beatrice!" he shouted. "I'm here! Your father is here!"

He scooped her up in his good arm and turned. The flames had closed the way behind him. He ran blindly toward the door anyway; the house stretched out before him, the flames grew hotter. His hair was burning, but he held Beatrice's head to protect her, even cradled his broken arm around her despite the pain. He hit a wall and bounced off and got turned around somehow. The flames were eating him. But he had to stay strong. Where was the door? He blinked several times. He spotted a square of light gleaming through the haze. He aimed for it.

A great *crack* shook the very air and he knew it was the frame of the house, its backbone breaking as it was consumed by the flames. A beam fell next to him. He leapt for the door only to have a fist the size of a steam tractor strike his back and pin him to the floor. He was right in the doorway, his arms and shoulders outside, the rest of him inside the house. He couldn't move. Nor could he feel his legs. He didn't know if the beam that had struck him had broken his back.

He opened his arms. At first he thought Beatrice wouldn't move, but she coughed and he shoved her and she rolled onto the front step, then into the grass and away from the house. She crawled a few feet, then turned her head to look back at him. She wasn't crying anymore and he was certain that she somehow understood what was happening. The flames were reflected in her eyes.

"Go," he whispered. "Go, little love. Go." He was blinking tears and now he felt the flames work their way up his body. But again he gritted his teeth to the pain and he watched his daughter struggling forward with each push of her legs. She was a survivor.

Horrible pain transfixed his body and he knew death was here, but his last thought was a comfort. *At least the smoke will bring the nieghbours. My daughters will be safe.*

Then Ernest Thorn took his final breath.

5

1926
Santa Monica, California

Late in the afternoon of August 28, Beatrice Thorn was standing at the window of the white stucco tower that overlooked the Cecil Estate. She wore khaki trousers, even though girls were supposed to wear dresses or bloomers. Her short-sleeved shirt kept her cool in the heat. Her notepad and pencil waited in her pocket. She didn't waste a moment staring down at the garden party below her, nor did she glance at the galaxy of birthmarks on her suntanned arms. Instead, she carefully pressed a pin through the thorax of a dead snipe fly, then forced the end of the long pin into the paper-covered corkboard resting on the windowsill. Beatrice examined her handiwork in the sunlight. The snipe fly was perfectly displayed—a fine addition to her insect collection. It even had some of her blood inside it. She set down the board and closed the lid on the killing jar, sealing in the sweet smell of chloroform.

"You done poking pins in flies?" Raul asked. His skin was dark, his eyes were dark, and so was his hair. He was seated in one of the school benches, his feet up on the desk. The knees of his white gardening clothes were stained green. She had known him since childhood, he was the only playmate she'd had other than her sister. Today he looked suddenly older—more like a young man. "It's absolutely boring."

An aggravating young man, Beatrice decided. "Boring! You're the one who interrupted my work. And you've made me wait while you finish a sketch."

"But that's different. It's art. And I'm an *artiste*. This is dead bugs."

"Go back to pruning palm trees with your father."

"What!" He pointed his index finger at her, wagging it playfully. "You invited me up here. Anytime, you said."

"Well, I couldn't just drop everything. Insects left in the killing jar get brittle." She placed the corkboard on the table. "Done. Done. Done."

Beatrice tightened the knot on the scarves that hid her nearly bald head. There were three scarves, in a variety of colours, and they were pulled against her skull like a second, silky skin. She couldn't hide the birthmarks scattered across her face, so she had declared a truce on her thoughts about them.

"Finally!" Raul clapped his hands. "Papá will be looking for me soon. What should we do for fun?"

"Tennis courts are off limits because of the party. So's the jungle gym and pool. I could read a book to you. I have a great one about the life cycle of butterflies."

"A book? Please—just poke my eyes out. Why don't we—"

A loud cheer rose up from far below the tower. Beatrice squinted down through the window. The Fancy Party That She Was Not Invited To was taking place in a green swath of garden only yards from the water. The cast and crew from Cecil Productions twirled and sashayed amongst the palm trees and Roman statues like a flock of underfed swans: white dresses, white hats, white suits. A chamber orchestra was doing its best to play jazz, providing the musical flavouring to each glorious moment. Six of the male actors were astride camels, attempting an awkward game of sand polo on the beach.

"Grasshoppers," she whispered. "They're all grasshoppers."

She couldn't help but wonder what it would be like to jump with them. Just once.

The party was a celebration of the production of another film. Tomorrow, the shooting would begin on *Frankenstein*. Today, they danced. Beatrice couldn't spot Isabelle in the gathering; she was probably still sleeping. Mr. Cecil wasn't there either. Knowing him, he was splicing film in his cottage home, which crouched in the shadow of the mansion. It had been built in a perfect circle. Even though Mr. Cecil was one of the richest men in California, he chose to live in a small place. Apparently all he needed was a bed and enough space to watch the dailies and splice film. Beatrice would love to go inside one day, but the cottage was verboten. No children were allowed in his sanctuary.

"How much longer should I make the chumps wait, Beets?" Isabelle said from the doorway.

Beatrice twitched in surprise, then turned. Her twin sister was in a shimmering black dress that seemed to be cut from a starry night sky. A cloche hat framed her immaculate face and a few blond curls peeked teasingly out of the bottom. Her silver shoes were high-heeled. Raul's eyes were wide.

Isabelle stepped into the room and did a twirl so that the gown of her dress umbrellaed out and in. The top of the dress fit tightly just below her clavicle, held up by thin straps that left her shoulders bare. She was very pale, despite the constant shining of the California sun. "I must be fashionably late by now."

"You can't be late for your own party," Raul whispered.

Isabelle gave a startled glance over her shoulder, but regained her composure in the blink of an eye. "Oh, your Mexican lovebird is here. How quaint. I thought he wasn't supposed to be in the house."

"He's not my *lovebird*," Beatrice growled. "He's my *friendbird*. And we don't always follow the rules."

Raul said nothing. His gaze was directed at Isabelle.

Beatrice thumped herself down in the wicker chair between the two of them and plopped her feet on the teak side table, purposely kicking Raul's leg. Hard. He rubbed it, but kept glancing back at Isabelle.

She patted her hair. "The party isn't just for me. It's for the other actors, too. There are camels. I asked for elephants! But I guess camels will do. You and your friendbird should come as a prince and princess. Get all dressed up. Ha! The more I think of it, the funnier that would be."

"Why would either of us want to go to that silly party?" Beatrice pretended to tighten the laces on her tennis shoes. "We're above it."

"Pshaw! You'd make a stunning pair. And oh . . . the gossip! Especially from the press-gallery boys. Maybe they'd finally stop writing about *moi*."

Beatrice rolled her eyes.

"I could drive both of you down the hill and smack dab into the middle of the party," Raul said. "In the delivery truck. I've driven it before. That'd be a ritzy entrance."

"Oh, you think big!" Isabelle took a step, reached down, and pinched his cheek with her gloved fingers. "It's what I like about you, Rauly-Pauly."

"Don't tease him," Beatrice said. "Neither of us can go. You know that."

"Come anyway. It's not fair you're not invited, Beets. It's a stupid rule. I mean that. I'm sick of you not being by my side." She put her hands on her hips. "Let's do it. Let's break the rules. Mr. Cecil won't stop me. He always lets me get my way at these shindigs."

Beatrice brushed her scarves off her shoulder. "The beautiful people would turn to stone at their first glimpse of me."

"That's not true," Isabelle said, slowly enough that she sounded unsure. She lowered her hand. "You could wear a mask. It would be so . . . so . . ."

"Daring?" Beatrice spouted. "Mysterious? Elizabethan?"

"Don't get testy, Beets."

"Oh, go talk your infantile talk and walk your infantile walk. They're your people—it's your world."

"And books and bugs and garden boys are *your* world!" Isabelle huffed. She stomped to the door and delivered her next words over her shoulder, "I am off, dear sister. I *am* off."

"Then be off," Beatrice said. "Off with your head. Off with the rest of you, too."

Isabelle's footsteps were already echoing on the marble stairs.

"Well, that was exciting." Raul rubbed his hands together. "Are you sure the two of you are twins?"

"Fraternal," she said. "We're dissimilar twins."

"You're more similar than you think."

She gave him a short, sharp glare. When she was younger this sort of comment might have led to fisticuffs. But the problem with fighting with the only other kid on the estate was that there'd be no one else to spend time with. Her sister was always at the studio.

There was another cheer from outside. Despite herself, Beatrice stood and went back to the window. Uncle Wayne waved his polo mallet around like a Saracen with a sword— celebrating a goal. He was legally the twins' guardian and, by blood, their cousin, but he and Betty preferred being called uncle and aunt. It had been that way since the girls were toddlers.

Isabelle was making her way down the stone path to the garden, holding the hem of her black dress in one hand. No one had noticed her yet. Then Aunt Betty turned expertly on her high heels and made a sweeping gesture toward Isabelle and the crowd applauded as the young actress performed a deep curtsy. *Applause just for arriving!* Beatrice thought. Even the orchestra joined in, adding pomp to the whole scene.

"Let's watch a flicker show," Beatrice said.

"Flicker show? Why do you keep using old words? They're movies now. Everyone calls them that."

Beatrice gave the party one more disdainful glance. "Because old words are invariably better. Do you want to watch one or not?"

"I'd rather go to the zoo."

"Off limits. The actors will be there teasing Mr. Lion. Showing the starlets how brave they are."

"Fine. A flicker show it is. You always get your way, don't you?" He smiled. She did like his smile.

"No. That's my sister," she said. "Now, let's go, Mr. Raul." She took his hand and pulled him toward the door.

6

Beatrice padded down the spiral tower staircase, her senses heightened by the possibility that they might be caught. Together. In the mansion. It had always been one of Mr. Cecil's rules that she and Raul could only play together outside. There was no explanation as to why this was a rule. Mrs. Madge, the governess, had eyes like an owl and relayed every single movement they made to Mr. Cecil. The punishment could be a week without seeing each other. Or two. Or worse, though Beatrice couldn't picture worse. She tiptoed to the bottom of the stairs and across the long hallway that led to the east wing of the mansion. Raul followed several steps behind.

"Have you ever worn a dress like your sister's?" he whispered.

"I don't wear dresses," she hissed. "Stop thinking about her."

"I was just curious. Like a cat."

"Can you be as quiet as one, too?"

She opened the thick door to the theater. Inside was seating for sixteen people. The velvet chairs were perfectly plush. Painted on one wall was a caveman-style drawing of a deer, on the opposite wall was the Roman Colosseum. The projector came out of the eye of a cyclops. The entire fourth wall was the screen.

Raul chose a seat near the centre of the front row. Beatrice clicked a brass-plated button on the floor. Several rooms away, in the servants' quarters, a bell rang. One of the servants made his way down the hall to the projector room. Since few of the house staff spoke English, Beatrice had never been able to learn any of their names—other than Zhen, the woman who ran the kitchen. There was new staff every month or so. Beatrice's theory about the frequent turnover was that they were easily worn out by Isabelle's demands.

"Which film will it be?" Raul whispered.

"Whatever's in the canister."

Mr. Cecil's collection was the finest in all of Hollywood, every reel of *The Birth of a Nation*, *The Phantom of the Opera*, *Sherlock, Jr.* (starring Buster Keaton), and thousands more. If Beatrice had wanted to, she could have watched her very arrival through the gates of the mansion—for there was expertly shot film of the long black car coming in the gates, then Uncle Wayne and Aunt Betty opening the doors and stepping out with two swaddled babes, which they handed to Mr. Cecil. He held them both, turning to show the camera his prizes. The idea that Mr. Cecil had hugged them in his arms was comforting. She had not left the estate since that day.

There was a clicking in the projection room, then the lights dimmed and the flickering began. The first thing to appear was the logo of Cecil Productions, a Rorschach ink-blot that Mr. Cecil had created. Beatrice shivered at the sight of it. *The unconscious projecting fear onto the stimuli of the image.* That was how Mr. Cecil had explained his odd logo. When someone saw it they felt fear. She'd studied these ink-blots with him on many occasions and they did make dark emotions rise to the surface.

The title came next: *Nosferatu's Blood.* It starred Isabelle and was about a vampire who had travelled from Transylvania to New York to dine on the rich. There was no music, as that was always provided in the theatre by a pianist or an orchestra. But Beatrice tapped her fingers rhythmically anyway.

The intertitles began: IN THE DARKEST LAND, THE DARKEST DEEDS ARE ABOUT TO OCCUR.

Beatrice didn't bother to read any more. She'd seen this film enough times that she had the text memorized. Uncle Wayne was a dashing vampire hunter and Aunt Betty his doting wife. Isabelle, their daughter, strode into the movie in a silken gown that made her look more vulnerable. Only a year younger than she was now. She glowed palely under the studio lights.

Beatrice imagined what it might be like to have those lights on you, to be in that other magical world that film showed to the human eye. It was all too possible to believe her sister had actually travelled to these places and experienced these adventures.

A whining like the sound a lost kitten might make came from the projection room. Beatrice turned her head, stared for a moment. The noise stopped and she fell back into the screen.

One by one the victims succumbed to Nosferatu until, at last, there was only her sister, running down the endless hallway of an ancient mansion, turning to scream and scream and scream. Silently. Her look of terror was utter and real.

Isabelle had become famous for that scream—in each of her last five films there'd been a similar scene. Audiences expected it. Desired it. They ate it up. The screams were practised at least once a week in what Mr. Cecil called Stanislavksi's Emotional Memory Release Sessions. Isabelle had taken to referring to them as the Screaming at the Top of Your Lungs Sessions. She was supposed to think about a horrible event from her childhood and scream. He often asked her to imagine what she had felt inside the burning farm house. Those feelings were still trapped inside her. Sometimes Isabelle would wear her voice down to a ragged rasp.

"She looks so different in real life," Raul whispered. "So much more real."

"You've seen her lots of times. In real life and on the screen."

"I know. It still surprises me."

"Nothing about her surprises me." Beatrice tightened her scarves again. "Would you like to watch another flicker show? Maybe *The Lost World*?"

"Father'll tear a strip off me if I miss any more work. Oranges to pick and all of that."

"We don't follow the rules, remember?"

"Papá's strap does. You've never had to sit on a burning bum, have you?"

"No. I guess not," she said. "Just tell him you were running away from Nosferatu."

He laughed.

A snuffling noise came from the projection room. Beatrice put her finger to her lips and snuck up to the hole where the projector poked out. She peeked through.

A young servant in a mandarin-collar shirt and black trousers was sitting on a stool, wiping tears from his face. The man looked up at Beatrice. His eyes widened and he stumbled out of the projection room, leaving the door open.

"What was it?" Raul asked.

"One of the Chinese was crying. Do you have any idea why?"

"Nope. Groundskeepers don't mix with the kitchen staff. Maybe Zhen shouted at him. She's terror on two legs."

"He might be homesick."

They left the theater and went into the India room, passing large golden elephants, statues of Indian gods, and a six-foot-tall replica of the Taj Mahal—all items Mr. Cecil had collected on his many journeys around the world.

She opened the window, stuck her head out, and looked around.

"The coast is clear," she said.

"Thank you, friendbird."

He punched her shoulder lightly, then slipped out the window and broke into a catlike run. He was soon past the hedge and out of sight.

Beatrice had spent ten thousand hours in the India room. And another ten thousand in the China room and twice that number in the Roman room. For the ten thousandth time she stared at a black marble statue of Ganesha, the god with the elephant head and four arms. She touched one of his hands.

A song began, as if someone had flicked on a phonograph. Beatrice held still. Was the marble growing warmer? Then she realized she'd left the window open. Someone at the party was singing "Bye Bye Blackbird"—no, not someone, it was Uncle Wayne. Soon a gaggle of other actors and actresses were joining in, each singing louder and louder. *Showing off, each and every one of them!*

Beatrice went back to the theatre and put her hand on the door. Another film would shut out the world.

But why watch her film sister while her real sister was in the garden?

I don't follow rules, she thought.

Beatrice may not have been invited to the party, but she could at least take a front-row seat. There would be "outside" people in the Pomona garden. It would be exotic. Like going on a safari.

A safari in her own backyard.

7

Weeks earlier Mr. Cecil had promised the world an "epic bash," and the *Frankenstein* soiree was more than fulfilling that promise. It was larger than the *Dark House* party and louder than the *Nosferatu's Blood* celebration. And it was ten times bigger than the party for the orphans. Beatrice got a chill when she thought of that celebration because it reminded her of Jolly.

She had discovered Jolly's body. The first to see her long hair spread out like a spiderweb in the Neptune pool. The first to touch her cold, cold arm. Beatrice put that fact—that sense memory—out of her mind. It was three years and two months ago. This was time to think of adventure.

She crept between the rows of hibiscus, crouched down when she reached the garden, and peered through the leaves of a lilac shrub. The musky scent of the ground drifted up. She stopped a few feet behind a long serving table. An angelic ice sculpture guarded one end of the table; glaring from the opposite end was a frozen Grim Reaper, his scythe raised for reaping. This was Mr. Cecil's sense of humour at work. If there were twenty skeletons in a scene he'd have one with a green polka-dot tie, identical to a tie worn by a director he didn't respect.

Beatrice took her pad of paper and a pencil out of her front pocket and noted every type of person she saw:

Actors (too many to list)
Actresses (too many to list)
Musicians
Three cameramen
Five reporters (the handsome one may be Robert Russel—love his writing!)
Mayor George Cryer (he looks like Buster Keaton!)
Senator Johnson
Archduke Leopold of Austria (wearing his military uniform)
Six male servants in black satin clothes (only one of them looks familiar)
Chips the trained monkey, in a vest . . .

The partygoers had seemed ridiculous from afar, but up close she was drawn by their beauty. And their need to be noticed. One starlet looked nervous, scratching at her frock. A male actor was sweating. It might actually be difficult to always be on show, Beatrice realized. And no matter how silly they sometimes seemed, every one of them breathed the air outside the walls of the Cecil Estate.

Uncle Wayne stood about fifteen feet away, dressed in a white suit with a top hat, his face shaved and smooth. He was speaking to a newspaperman wearing a fedora, with a pad of paper and fountain pen in hand. Wayne clapped the man on his shoulder and flashed his smile. It was full of light and perfect teeth, the sword he'd used to conquer the world.

The orchestra, which had been playing softly in the background, began to pound a dramatic symphonic piece that drowned out the conversations. The music hit a crescendo followed by a sudden fall into silence.

"A toast to our brightest star, Isabelle Thorn!" The director's deep voice cut through the garden air. Mr. Cecil was seated on the back of an obsidian statue of a three-headed lion, holding a full flute of champagne in his right hand. It was as if he'd popped out of nowhere. He wore a dark suit with golden buttons and a white panama hat—the combination of the straw hat and his attire made him look like a businessman and an adventurer. His hair was brown but dappled with white, and his grey eyes seemed to be cataloguing every morsel of information as he looked around. The only noticeable imperfection was that he was missing the little finger on his left hand. He'd once told Beatrice and Isabelle that he'd gambled it away in a game of cards in which his opponent had lost his whole hand and now used a hook to smoke his cigarettes.

The actors quickly grabbed their own flutes and shouted, *"Hip, hip hooray, Isabelle! Hip, hip hooray!"* The light glinted off the glasses as they sipped their champagne in unison. Isabelle curtsied and pretended to blush. A photographer's flashbulb brightened all of their faces.

"I'll be a man of few words," Mr. Cecil continued. "I know you'll be pleased to hear that." There were a few muffled laughs. "We came. We saw. We conquered the cinematic world. *The Dark House* is the greatest movie we've made. And within a month of its release it has become our most lucrative. A toast to all who worked so hard to make that film a reality."

The audience drank again. Mr. Cecil didn't drink from his glass—Beatrice had never seen him drink or eat. She chalked this up to the fact that he was immensely rich. The rich could indulge whatever eccentricities they wanted.

"I know you'll rise to the challenge of our next project, *Frankenstein*. We will be the first to reach the high-water mark of film production. We'll create an intelligent and beautiful movie that sets the industry on its ear." He chuckled. "In other words, we'll have sound in our film." He let the statement hang in the air. "Yes, you can write that down, you scribblers! Sound! Finally." He paused. "There. Speech done. Drink, eat, and be very merry. Tomorrow we will write our names in history."

There was more applause. Mr. Cecil bowed slightly, then hopped to the ground. He was immediately surrounded by actors and newspapermen, all wanting a word.

Beatrice spotted a plate of cream puffs at the edge of the table and licked her lips. She could get a cream puff any hour of the day, but these ones were intended for the guests. Not her. Not ever. It would be daring to take the whole plate. No, that would be greedy! But a handful would be enough. And yet, once she came out from behind the lilac bush she'd be spotted.

Isabelle had sashayed closer to the table with her *I'm almost pouting* face on. At that moment no one was talking to her—even the photographers were snapping pictures of Mr. Cecil. *Turn, Isabelle, turn,* Beatrice thought. She stared directly at the back of her sister's head. So often they seemed to think the same thought at the same time: this was the ten thousandth time she'd tried to send her own thought into Isabelle's head. *Izzy! Izzy! Turn and bring me the cream puffs.* Maybe the cloche hat was blocking the signal. She squinted hard. *I command thee!*

Nothing. *So much for the secret perception between twins,* she thought. *Perhaps it has to be an angry thought.*

Izzy! Get me a damn cream puff!

Isabelle turned and looked directly at Beatrice. She winked, went to the table, and gently grasped a handful of cream puffs. Then she backed up, her right hand resting on her spine. There were three cream puffs in her palm.

Beatrice snatched them with barely even the lightest touch on her sister's hand. Then came a quiet and delighted laugh, whether it was hers or her sister's she wasn't certain.

We got away with it!

Beatrice drew in a breath. Mr. Cecil was staring at her through a break in the crowd, his face a mask. She couldn't determine what emotion he was displaying: anger or contemplation? A smile came slowly to his lips.

She smiled in return, pulled back into the leaves, and quickly swallowed one of the cream puffs. She clutched the other two gently in her left hand and climbed the terraced garden, all the while keeping herself hidden.

When she was high enough she darted over to the vineyard. It was late August, not yet harvest season, but dark grapes were already dangling from the vines. She followed the straight line of trellises until she was able to cross upward to the row of orange trees and finally climb the southwest path.

Her safari was finished. She sighed as she walked out of the cover of the bushes, only a few steps from the mansion.

"What's your name?" a man asked.

She turned, looking over her shoulder in such a way as to hide much of her face. The man in the fedora hat was leaning up against the stucco wall of the mansion. He had a pad of paper in one hand and a pen in the other.

"It's a simple question, miss. What's your name?"

8

"Umm," Beatrice said. "Umm."

"Ah, you can talk." The newspaperman had a kindly thin face, though his eyes were alert and focused on her. His hair was dark and short. A small black feather decorated his fedora. She'd already labelled him as the most handsome of the reporters. "I saw you hiding in the bushes at the party. Watching all the silliness. I'm just asking your name. That's not so much to ask for, is it? My name's Robert Russel."

Beatrice blinked. His name was all too familiar. He'd mentioned her three times in his articles about Isabelle, as the mysterious twin sister. And always there would be a line about how her mother had died giving birth to her, the farmhouse that had burned down, and how her father had died saving her. It made her sound like a walking bad-luck charm. "I'm—I'm Beatrice."

"And do you have a last name?"

"Thorn."

"Aha." Triumph flashed in his eyes. "So you exist. I thought Mr. Cecil was yanking my chain all these years. I wish McRoberts was here to snap your pic, but he's too busy with the so-called stars. The real story is standing right in front of me."

"I don't want my picture taken." She still hadn't turned completely around. Beatrice hid the bottom half of her face in the crook of her arm.

"That makes you a breath of fresh air. Every dame within sight of the Hollywood Hills wants to pose for pictures." He blew air between his lips, making a horselike sound. "You can lower your arm. I won't be taking any snapshots."

She did so and turned toward him. He eyed her without any sign of discomfort, as if he had expected to see the birthmarks and her irregular-shaped face. Perhaps as a reporter he'd seen worse things.

"Your scarves are spectacular," he said. "So colourful."

She touched one of them. "They're from Paris."

"I'm not surprised. Have you been there?"

She shook her head. Felt her scarves move on her shoulders.

"I have. Once. Tried to write a novel and failed miserably. But I write for the *New York Times* now." He said this with pride, seemed to stand a bit straighter. "The Russel Hollywood Report. Have you heard of it?"

"Of course. I—I've read your writing."

"You've read me? You have exquisite taste." His laugh was gentle. "How old are you?"

"Twelve."

"Same age as Isabelle, of course. It's like I've stumbled on a unicorn."

"A unicorn? Have you been drinking?" she blurted. Then she covered her mouth.

"I never touch the stuff at work. And I have a hundred million questions. I mean, are you really from that farm up north? With the house that burned down, leaving you an orphan? Is all of that true?"

"I'm not supposed to answer any questions."

He slapped himself on the forehead. "Oh, sorry—stupid me. I completely understand. Then let's you and I just chat. You likely don't talk to too many people. That's my guess. I got my job by being a good guesser. 'Hunches' we call them in the business."

"I don't trust hunches," she said. "I construct theories and then I test them."

"A regular Marie Curie." Beatrice puffed up a bit. She'd often made imaginary scientific discoveries side by side with an imaginary Marie Curie.

Russel jerked his thumb toward the party. "You and me, we don't belong here. I'm just a reporter. I'll never be a star like them. And you . . . well, you aren't one of them either. You're . . ." He searched for the right word.

Ugly, Beatrice thought.

". . . smarter than them. We have that in common. So maybe we could just chat like old pals."

"I don't have any pals." Immediately she realized she was wrong. Raul was her friend. And so was Jolly. Well, she was dead and you couldn't be friends with the dead. And Beatrice had never actually spoken with her. But they could have been friends if the situation had been different.

"Ha! In the news biz you don't have any friends either. Just contacts and sources and stories to dig up."

"It must be very interesting work." He did have attractive green eyes, she decided. Trustworthy eyes.

"On days like today it's interesting. Right now. But mostly it's sifting through the manure people want you to believe and trying to find out what really happened. It takes a lot of digging to find the truth."

"I try to find the truth, too. And breakthroughs. Scientific ones." The cream puffs were melting in her hand. A cry of joy came from The Party She Was Not Invited To—it sounded like Aunt Betty. Beatrice tightened her grip.

"Speaking of breakthroughs, did you know any of the orphans?" Robert Russel asked.

"The orphans? No. No. I didn't."

"Do you know where they went?"

"No."

He took out his pen as if he were going to write something down, then slipped it back into his pocket. "Sorry. I have this annoying habit of writing everything down."

"I do, too." She pulled out her own pad of paper and her pencil.

"A girl after my own heart."

Something about the black feather in his fedora made her think of Peter Pan. He did look young for a grown-up. "It's a good habit to write things down," she said.

"Yes. I suppose it is. I was asking about the orphans because the story of that girl drowning got the soft treatment. It was sold as if Mr. Cecil had lost his own daughter.

But I'm a stickler for details. Thought I'd get the orphans' point of view. I went looking for the kids from Cecil's institute the next day to interview them. I couldn't find a single one. Not even a strand of hair. And I'm damn—I mean darn—good at finding people. But for the orphanage to close up shop and for all of them to disappear was rather curious."

"I didn't know any of them." She slid her pad of paper back into her pocket. "I don't know where they went."

"Thanks for answering me, anyway." He motioned toward the mansion and up to the tower above them. "It's rather amazing what Absalom has built here."

"Who?" she asked.

"Absalom Cecil. You mean you didn't know his first name? No one seems to know it. I had to sift through a million dusty property records to find that out. It's curious that he doesn't use his first name."

"He has good reasons for everything. He's a really smart man. He notices everything." She bit her lip. *He might somehow be able to see me right now.* "It's been very pleasant talking to you, Mr. Russel."

"You don't want to talk anymore?"

"I'm supposed to be inside."

"Oh, is that some kind of rule or something? A law?"

She nodded.

"Well, it shouldn't be that way. A girl with a brain like yours should be out in the world."

"This—this brain has to go now." She was proud of that. A clever statement.

"I won't stand in your way. I really appreciate your speaking with me." Then he gave her a smile that looked like he really meant the following words: "I'd like to chat again, Beatrice. We all need people to talk to in the world. Just look me up."

"How?"

"Write me care of the *New York Times.*"

"I'm not allowed to do that."

"Ah, I see. Then I'll find a way to get a message to you. I'm good at that sort of secretive spy thing. Just to say hello and check up on my new pal."

Her heart was beating fast. "I'd like that. And . . . I look forward to reading your writing. It's good."

"That's a high compliment. Thanks. Take care, Miss Beatrice Thorn."

She walked away, went in the south door, and slowly climbed the stairs of the white stucco tower—La Torre Blanca. The words from the conversation followed her with every step.

9

Three floors of books—walls made of words and ideas—rose above Beatrice along the open spiral staircase. The tower stairwell also served as the mansion's main library and she'd read nearly the entire collection. All of her favourite thinkers were there: Archimedes, Marie Curie, Henry David Thoreau. There were novels, too, and history and mythology books.

She stopped in the education quarters, a term Mr. Cecil had given the room. He'd even had it set up like a prairie school, with row desks, a blackboard, and a larger desk for Mrs. Madge. It was all done that way, he'd explained, so they'd remember their simple roots and how far they'd come. Beatrice spun the globe with one hand as she passed it, then sat at her chair and laid the remaining cream puffs on top of her teak study desk.

She pulled out her notebook and wrote: *Can Mr. R. really be my pal?* He was a young man, but far too old to be friends with her. It wasn't like he'd want to play cards or go for a swim. Maybe they could have a game of tennis. No, she realized, they'd likely never meet again. Unless there was another party and he found her in one of her hiding spots. Or if he was somehow able to get a message through to her.

She stuffed a cream puff in her mouth and ate it in one gushy bite.

"Does the second one taste better than the first?"

Mr. Cecil was in the doorway holding a paper bag in one hand.

"Oh. Hello." She palmed the final cream puff and closed her notebook. "How—how are you, today?"

"I'm exceptionally well, Beatrice. Nothing like a party to get the nerve endings tingling. But I'm curious as to why you made an appearance at my little soiree."

"I didn't." He raised an eyebrow. "I mean no one saw me. So I wasn't really there."

"I saw you. And I'm not no one."

Beatrice scratched her earlobe. "I'm sorry, Mr. Cecil. I should've stayed inside."

He crossed the room, still clutching the bag, and set it in front of her. He was handsome. Not movie-star handsome like her uncle, but he had a solidity to his presence and appearance. "It's my fault, Beatrice. I've been making too many rules for you. Did you feel excluded?"

"Not really. I mean—I didn't work on the film and I'm not an actor."

"We're all actors. It's a survival skill. Did you come on a dare from your sister?"

"I—I just wanted to be closer to everything, that's all."

"Almost like a safari in your own backyard." It was as if he'd plucked the words from her mind. "You're growing up.

It's what young girls do. You need to grow outward, and test the edges. Like a butterfly emerging from its pupa. We all go through our metamorphosis, some for the better, some for the worse. Why, if you'd seen me in the earliest stages of my life—let's say the larva stage—you'd be surprised at how different I was. Unrecognizable. And how much I've changed since."

"You were never a larva worm. I just can't see it."

"I was. Perhaps I still am. Waiting to emerge." He let out a friendly laugh. "I can only have these types of jokingly scientific conversations with you, Beatrice. No one else on this estate has a mind as brilliant as yours."

The words hung in the air for a few moments. Beatrice didn't blush.

"Anyway," Mr. Cecil continued. "I sense you're tired of being trapped in this tower."

"I—I like the tower," she said. "It's my home. It's all I've ever known." She let those last words hang in the air. She wasn't certain whether they were a complaint or a statement.

"I've been far too busy on this last film. I wish I could slow the world down and play a game of chess with you. Maybe in the India room like we did only a few months ago. Would you like that?"

"Yes. Yes, of course!"

"Then it'll happen after *Frankenstein* is done." He patted her on the shoulder. "It's not enough for you to be your sister's pillar, is it?"

"No, I guess not."

"But nothing has changed outside these walls. The actors—all of my employees—I trust them. They've signed their contracts. But the newspaper people are leeches. Did any of them talk to you?"

"No, no one." She lowered her eyes.

"Good," he said. "They want to bring the mighty down and make us all as petty as them. You're not unattractive, but they would paint you as a monstrous replica of your sister—as a Medusa." She had read the myth of Medusa several hundred times—a beautiful woman turned into a snake-haired monster by the jealous goddess Minerva. The sight of Medusa would turn onlookers to stone. But even Medusa had her own strength. And she had sisters. "I'll do everything in my power to save you the pain of reading those hurtful words."

"I don't waste much time on the papers." She paused. "Well, I do read about Isabelle." *And myself,* she could have added.

"Remember Fatty Arbuckle?" Mr. Cecil said. "The papers accused him of being involved in that young actress's death. He was acquitted, but the reporters and the public had already convicted him. People want to believe the worst story."

Fatty had been one of the funniest and most popular actors in the film world. Beatrice loved his movie *The Cook*, with Buster Keaton. When a young actress died in his hotel room under mysterious circumstances his name was plastered across the front page of every paper in America. "I—I don't want to work in the movies," Beatrice said.

"I want to protect you. But I should give you more of a

role in your own life. And I'll proudly show you to the world when the time is right. You'll leap out of your cocoon and have your debut! When we can control the story, that is. Will you promise to follow my rules until that time?" She nodded slowly. He put his left hand on her shoulder. Despite his missing finger, the grip was strong and warm and compelling. "Your words are your bond, Beatrice. Speak them."

"I promise, Mr. Cecil."

"Good girl." He smiled. It was not the stars-in-the-sky smile of her uncle. It was much more subtle. "We're alike, you and I. We collect things. I collect pieces of art, pieces of history to remind me of what I've seen. I collect actors, too. And you collect insects and ideas. We are both survivors: I came from the old country and built all of this from nothing. You come from nothing, too. If it was possible for me to have a daughter I'd want it to be you."

Adopt me, she almost said. "You've been so good to me. To us. You're my other father."

"That's extremely kind of you to say. I did bring a gift."

He motioned at the paper bag. Beatrice grabbed it and thrust her hand in the top. "It's empty."

"It depends on where you look." In his right hand he was holding a rectangular box wrapped in gold foil.

"Misdirection. A magician's greatest skill."

His grin was genuine. "Yes. Forgive me. I do sometimes miss my simple days of being Cecil the Magnificent in *The Wondrous and Amazing Travelling Excitements Show.* Ah, my younger years have fled. Watch over my gift and it will watch over you." He patted her head. "And don't forget to have that final cream puff." He winked, then strode out of the room without a backward glance.

The box was so expertly wrapped that it was seamless. It took Beatrice several moments to find an edge to the gold foil so she could unfold it. Inside was a framed insect. The unfamiliar specimen looked like an elongated hornet with large clear wings and the tail of a scorpion. There was a skull-and-crossbones pattern on the wings. Its compound eyes reflected a hundred Beatrices.

Mr. Cecil had brought her a rare insect!

She stuffed the last cream puff in her mouth. The sugary goodness spilled out onto her tongue, but she was too busy examining her new prize to notice.

10

The moon rose and the *Frankenstein* bash continued into the silver-lit darkness. The orchestra's playing was no longer crisp and perfect. Drunken singing, along with a cool breeze, drifted along the tops of the palm trees and through the open window of the twins' bedroom in the west wing of the mansion.

Isabelle sighed. "I guess the party doesn't end when I leave." She had changed into a pink nightgown with gold lace trim and combed out her long flaxen hair, and was now filing her nails in bed, her feet up on a pillow.

"It's turning into a catastrophic cacophony." Beatrice set the August issue of *Scientific American* down. "By now Aunt Betty and Uncle Wayne must be truly sauced."

"They were sauced before I left, along with everyone else. Me, I need my beauty sleep. And you have no idea how painful dress shoes are." She wriggled her toes. Each toenail was painted hot pink. "My feet are killing me."

"They smell like they're already dead."

"Beets! That's no way to talk. These are the feet a thousand actresses would kill to have." She brandished one toward her sister. "Rub them for me."

"Not on your life!"

Another toe wriggle followed. "I'll get Rauly-Pauly to rub them. Doesn't he rub yours?"

Beatrice smacked her with the magazine. "No!"

"I'm just curious what you two get up to when I'm not around."

"That's none of your business."

Isabelle giggled her actress giggle. "Aw, don't get your dukes up, sis. It's funny, isn't it, how his mom died in that farm accident—"

"She had cancer."

"Yes, that's right. But she died and he ended up here with his father. And we ended up here after our mom died, too. Well, and our father." It wasn't the first time Isabelle had mentioned this connection between their story and Raul's, and Beatrice was certain she knew what was coming next. "Do you think it's fate? That our lives were . . . were meant to be this way?"

"There's no such thing as fate," Beatrice said. "There is just a series of things happening that look like they're fated. But it's all numbers."

"Oh, you and that brainy brain of yours. Always letting the air out of all the fun in a room."

"It's just logic."

"Well, I'm glad you have Raul to keep your brain occupied. It'd be wonderful to frolic around the grounds like you kids. But I have scripts to memorize, cameras to pose for, and reporters to wow with my cleverness."

"I bet that last bit takes the most work."

"Ha! I'm a natural." She flipped her hair back. "They find my wittiness both droll and charming. They fall all over themselves at the press gallery. You have no idea what that's like."

"I'm sure they're amazed that a hot-air balloon like you can even talk." Before her sister could give her a playful slap she added: "You're not the only one to chat with the press."

"What do you mean?"

"Nothing—I don't mean anything."

"No." Isabelle repeatedly poked Beatrice with her index finger. "You're keeping a secret, Beets. You can't keep secrets from me. Tell me. Tell me, now."

Beatrice used the magazine to ward off her sister's finger. "Promise not to speak a word of it?"

"I promise a thousand times over."

"One of the reporters tracked me down. Robert Russel."

"Rob?" Isabelle waved her hand as if the heat had gone up in the room. "Handsome, isn't he? I mean, for a reporter."

"Well, no . . . yes. I guess so."

"He's one of the important ones. He has his own column." Isabelle made a kissy face. "Did you smooch him?"

"What? No! He's too old."

"You're blushing, dear sister."

"I'm angry."

"What did you two talk about?"

"Nothing." Beatrice hugged her pillow. "Well, he asked about the orphans. Jolly and all the other ones."

"Oh. That was a million years ago."

"It was three years."

"Nine movies ago. And Jolly was mouthy. She had her own opinions about things. And she was nosy, too."

"Nosy? About what?"

"Oh, she asked me too many questions about Mr. Cecil." Isabelle switched to a falsetto voice. "'Where is he from?' she asked me. 'Old musty Europe,' I said. 'How did he lose his finger?' 'In a card game.' That stumped her. Ha! Get it? 'And what does Mr. Cecil eat?' She even asked that."

"Maybe she had a scientific mind."

"A nosy-posy mind. Anyway, why would ol' Rob ask about them?"

"He said the orphans vanished after the orphanage was closed."

Isabelle shrugged. "I'm sure Mr. Cecil found homes for them, that's all. Well, except Jolly, of course. That part was kind of sad." She sniffed slightly. "Did the mighty Robert Russel have anything else to say?"

"He said I was a unicorn."

"Wow. What a line."

Beatrice ran her fingers along the cover of the magazine. It was an image of a man with a telescope. "It wasn't a line. He was happy to find me."

"Don't let Mr. Cecil know Rob saw you. He likes to keep a close eye on those reporters. And you. And me. And, well, everything. He's—"

There was a knock on the door. "Sorry to bother you," Mr. Cecil said. "May I come in?"

"En-tray vooz!" Isabelle answered without missing a beat.

Mr. Cecil opened the door. A nocturnal visit was not unusual, for he had read to them when they were younger. The fact that he'd left the party to see them must mean it was important. The sisters sat up.

"My talented darlings," Mr. Cecil said. "I'm sorry to intrude. I've read how twins need togetherness time."

"It's no bother," Isabelle said. "Beatrice and I were just gabbing."

"Ah, gabbing is great practice for an actress." He glanced over at the wall. "And Beatrice, you've hung up my gift! Wonderful."

"Yes," Beatrice said. "I plan on studying it every morning. What's its scientific classification and where did it come from?"

"Those are mysteries I'll leave your inquisitive mind to discover."

"Why are you bringing her gifts and not me?" Isabelle asked. "I mean . . . don't feel like you have to get me a bug. But pearls would be nice."

"Well, I come with pearls of wisdom. Tomorrow will be a great odyssey into the world of *Frankenstein*. Beatrice, I'll be taking your sister with me. Do I have your permission?"

"Yes. Just bring her back in one piece."

"I will. I must deliver on my promise of releasing the first film with sound." He placed his hand on Isabelle's shoulder. "And that means that you, Isabelle, will have to act with even more depth and authenticity than ever before. It'll be a trial."

Isabelle saluted. "Private Thorn reporting for duty."

Mr. Cecil returned her salute. "You both have bravery in spades. But I want to put a coat of armour on you like Joan of Arc's. Please get out of bed."

Isabelle stepped onto the floor. She came up to Mr. Cecil's shoulder. It was as if she'd grown several inches during the course of the party. The hem of her nightgown hung an inch below her knees.

"Did you know that once upon a time I was a mesmerist?" Mr. Cecil said.

"Was that after you were a magician?" Beatrice asked.

"Oh, it was years before that. And long before Freud and Jung began using hypnotism to explore the subconscious. I would unlock people to help them discover their inner potential. All I used was this simple tool." A golden watch on a chain appeared in his hand. "Train your eyes on the watch, the pendulum of time, the moments slipping by ever more slowly. Slowly. Slowly. They are drops of water in a vast ocean. Future. Past. Present. Each together. Each one."

Isabelle was quiet, her lips tight as she gazed at the watch, and Beatrice herself could not stop staring at the pendulum-like movement. "Future. Past. Present. Each together. Each one," he repeated. His voice grew as soft as the sound of falling grains of sand. "The doorways inside you are opening as I count. Ten. Nine. Eight. Seven."

Beatrice blinked—it was the slowest blink she'd ever experienced. When her eyes opened again time had skipped ahead. Her sister was as immobile as a butterfly in amber. And Mr. Cecil was looking at her and at Beatrice at the same time as though he had two faces.

Janus, Beatrice thought. *The god with two faces. The god of doorways. Of openings.*

She blinked a second time. Mr. Cecil was whispering into Isabelle's right ear. Beatrice strained to hear. He continued to stare at Beatrice with his second face and he did not blink. *All animals have to blink,* she thought.

Then a blank space.

Beatrice shook her head, a slow, slow motion. The pendulum watch had stopped swinging. She blinked again at full speed and Mr. Cecil now had only one face.

"You are unlocked," he said to Isabelle. "You will become Rosella Frankenstein. Now wake, wake, wake, my dear, and join the world. Your armour is on."

Isabelle opened her eyes. Her knees gave out and Mr. Cecil gently grabbed her under the arms. "Sit on the bed. Sleep, child. Tomorrow is the start of a grand adventure and you'll need your rest."

He helped her into bed, then tucked her in and playfully shook his finger at Beatrice. "I almost had you, too, didn't I? You felt time slow."

"Yes."

"But you kept your own thoughts."

She hesitated. "Yes."

"Interesting. Very interesting. Tomorrow, time will speed up. We'll be filming as many hours as possible to meet the deadline. You'll need your forty winks, my dears. Sleep well. Sleep. 'Sleep, perchance to dream.'"

He bowed slightly and left the room, closing the door behind him.

"I feel different," Isabelle said. "All charged up. I'm more alive."

Beatrice wasn't certain what she felt. Mr. Cecil couldn't have altered time. Her mind did sometimes play tricks on her—when she was reading a book or watching a film, time seemed to slow down.

She could not stop her eyes from closing.

She awoke, moments later, to screaming. Beatrice snapped open her eyes and shot into a sitting position, her heart hammering against her chest. She turned, for she was certain it was Isabelle who was screaming, but her sister was lying as calm and serene as a figure in a mausoleum. One lone dot of perspiration rested on her forehead.

It must have been inside my head, Beatrice thought.

There was a long groan outside, then a wail, then laughter. The party wasn't dead yet. But it was getting quieter and the music was done, replaced by the endless lapping of the waves on the beach.

Beatrice listened to the waves. It took her a long time to sleep.

11

The next morning at five her sister, uncle, aunt, and Mr. Cecil took the Lincoln Town Car to the studio. Beatrice found the energy to stand at the window and wave, then she returned to bed. She woke up again at seven and dressed, pausing when she opened her drawer of the dresser she shared with Isabelle. Inside that drawer was a picture of her father, and a few of his war medals, but on the very top was a collection of coloured-pencil drawings that Raul had made: a rose, a monarch butterfly, and one image of her scarves. He had not drawn the scarves flat on the desk like she'd asked, but had composed them as if they were around her head. Her face was blank. She looked like an invisible woman. Or as if she could have any face.

She set the drawing down, grabbed a pair of stockings, and pulled on her shoes. She ate breakfast alone. It was a school day, which meant that Mrs. Madge, the governess, taught her mathematics and science. She was a woman who was all angles and straight lines: her cheekbones; her thin, wiry arms; her lack of discernible hips. And she delivered her material in a drone.

Later, Beatrice filled the afternoon looking for insects and making faces at Raul as he worked alongside his father.

By evening, she had two thoughts on her mind: *How is Izzy doing?* and *Did Robert Russel's report on the party come out?* But the mail was late, and it wasn't until after seven that a mechanical buzzing indicated the delivery boy was rumbling down the road on his motorized bicycle. Beatrice slipped out of the house and stepped into the shadow behind a large planter decorated in Roman patterns. She peered through the ferns. The boy putted up to the front door, jumped off his bicycle, leaned it against a column, and flipped back his goggles. He was a gawky long-armed kid with red hair and a flat nose. He took their mail and a package of newspapers out of his saddlebag and set both in the gold-plated mailbox. Then he got on his bike and glanced in Beatrice's direction.

She ducked and held her breath until she heard the bike start up and the delivery boy *put, put* back down the road.

Beatrice leapt up to the mailbox. She pushed aside the cloth bag that would have a portion of Isabelle's fan mail in it (a young woman in a studio office answered the rest of it, including signing photographs to be mailed to fans; Isabelle had even received a letter from President Calvin Coolidge once). There was a smaller pile of letters for Uncle Wayne, including one with a red lipstick kiss on it and three or four fan letters addressed to Aunt Betty.

Beatrice snuck the *New York Times* out of the stack of papers. She then slipped into the China room and sat on the bamboo bench next to a giant jade dragon. She took a deep, long draught of air and opened the newspaper.

What if he mentions me?

Well, she decided, that would be a disaster. But she would finally be more than *Oh, and Isabelle has a twin sister whom no one sees.* She would be stepping out, so to speak. In words at least.

It occurred to her that perhaps, just perhaps, Robert Russel would communicate directly to her through his report. Using words that would have a secret meaning for her. Maybe he'd say something about seeing a unicorn. Or about a wonderful young woman with the most amazing scarves. It couldn't be too much of a mention, because then Mr. Cecil would guess they really had talked. Just enough to let people know she'd been at the party! That she was real.

Her heart thumped a little harder when she flipped to his article.

The New York Times
Saturday, August 30, 1926

The Russel Hollywood Report
Great Big Grand Party to Announce the First Sound Film from Cecil Productions

The party at the Cecil Estate was big. It was grand. And it had one of the biggest announcements in Hollywood history ever.

Mr. Cecil of Cecil Productions will have sound in his next film. Sound! Isn't that amazing?

The film will be called *Frankenstein* and
stars twelve-year-old Isabelle Thorn, already
a big star, as the daughter of Frankenstein.
It guest stars Wayne Michaels (who is her real-
life guardian).

Beatrice paused. The writing wasn't as interesting as his
usual fare. He'd said that he never touched alcohol at work,
but maybe he'd broken his own rule and this boring prose
was the best his fuzzy brain could come up with.

"It'll be the first popular film to use sound,"
Mr. Cecil announced to a crowd of big stars and
celebrities, including Mayor George Cryer of
Los Angeles and Archduke Leopold of Austria.
"It will set the world on its ear."
The popular director is a very funny man.
Isabelle Thorn herself was there in a very
special black dress (the other actors all wore
white). There was also an orchestra and a game of
polo played on camels. Camels! Only in Hollywood!
The party was declared a grand success (such a
success that Robert Russel is yet to return from
the party, which is why I, William MacRoberts,
cameraman, am filing this story—if anyone has
seen him, turn his mug in our direction and send
him home).

Beatrice dropped the paper on the floor. *Too drunk to write his own article!*

"So unprofessional," she hissed. An image of her stomping on the paper flashed in her mind, but she chose not to make it reality. *Maybe when he finally sobers up, he'll write something worth reading.*

She decided to pick up the paper. The article still belonged in the scrapbook. She put the *Times* under her arm and walked into the front hallway.

The door opened and Mongo, in his grey driving suit, was standing there. Which meant her sister was finally home. The Lincoln Town Car was behind him in the driveway.

He nodded at Beatrice, mute as always. *The walking tongueless mountain,* Beatrice thought.

It was a mystery she had not been able to solve: Why had Mongo's tongue been cut out?

1. He had taken part in an ancient secret ritual.
2. He had seen something he shouldn't have. A murder.
3. He had a cancer.

One must examine all possibilities. It was the scientific method.

Isabelle, Aunt Betty, and Uncle Wayne climbed out of the car. Isabelle leaned on Betty's shoulder as they walked up to the main door.

"Welcome back, weary travellers," Beatrice said.

Isabelle took three steps into the mansion and threw herself onto the nearest leather armchair, her blue dress splayed across her legs. "Ah, what a day—I'm beat! Mongo, carry me to bed."

The driver took a lumbering step toward her and Isabelle rolled her eyes. "I was kidding, you monstrous brute. Go back to your cave." Without a change in his facial expression, he nodded and left, closing the door gently behind him.

"Ah, Beets," Isabelle said. "I command thee to carry me to bed."

"Sure! One body part at a time, starting with your head."

"Beatrice!" Aunt Betty said. "Don't joke about that." She was clutching her mail, which she had retrieved from the side table.

"Oh, Auntie, don't get cross." Isabelle waved her hand. "Beets has an odd-duck sense of humour. She spends her time pulling the legs off bugs."

Uncle Wayne wagged his index finger. "Help your sister, Beatrice. She worked hard. Get her a glass of water."

"We have servants for that," Beatrice said. "I just want to know how the day went."

"Hard." Isabelle let another sigh escape her body. "Good night, Auntie. Beets will see all my body parts to bed."

"Well, I have pictures to sign and that sort of thing. You aren't the only star in this house, Izzy." Aunt Betty patted the side of her head to be sure her hair was still in place. She had enough coconut oil in it that it wouldn't move until long after she was dead. "Remember, Beatrice. Isabelle needs her sleep.

Make sure she gets it. There's another big day tomorrow."
Her shoes *click-clacked* as she walked toward the east wing.

"You reading the reports on the party?" Uncle Wayne
asked, pointing at the paper under her arm.

"No. Just the science articles."

"Ha, right," he said. "I forgot who I was talking to. They
could have filled the whole paper with party news. I was the
last man standing. Not even the gaffers could outdrink me.
It was the best bash of the year. The best ever. I was still half
ossified this morning."

"I should've been allowed to stay up until the end,"
Isabelle said.

"There are things little girls shouldn't see. Even the
newspaper men were blotto. That snot from New York tried
to drink me under the table. He failed. It's the oldest trick in
the book: get the actor drunk and get him to spill his beans.
He machine-gunned me with questions about both of you."

"He asked about me?" Beatrice said. Isabelle gave her
a wink.

"Oh, he was sniffing he was. But I kept talking nonsense
until he passed out. New Yorkers can't hold their alcohol,
it's a known fact. I grew up on the strongest hooch in existence—Lethbridge Lightning. Speaking of that, I think I need
another hair of the dog." He walked down the hall.

Isabelle let out a third sigh. "Neither of them did much
today but complain about their headaches. I had to find the
scenic truth that Mr. Cecil keeps barking about."

"It's harder at the beginning of a shoot, isn't it?"
Beatrice said.

"Yes. It's like I have to learn to act all over again." Isabelle held out her hand. "Help me up. I need sleep. Real sleep." Beatrice guided her up the stairs to their room.

"I'm so glad I have you," Isabelle said. "You're always so . . . so solid."

"I'm made of flesh."

"And plain, too. Plain-speaking, I mean." In the light of the room it was clear that Isabelle's whitening greasepaint had not all been washed off. "It's going to be a grand film, Beets."

"You say that every time."

"I suppose I do. But Mr. Cecil has outdone himself this time. You know the big hangar studio? He built a castle inside. It's as if you're walking into the olden days. There's fog and a bright red electric moon and everything. And the castle has courtyards and stuff. And he's switched to inkies."

"Inkies?"

"Incandescent lights. They don't hum, so the sound won't be picked up on the Cinétone. And the makeup has to be all different for the lights. It's cutting edge." She wiped at her eyelid, smudging her eyeshadow. "Help me get my shoes off." She put her feet up on the bed.

"Take your own shoes off."

Isabelle kicked off her black shoes and wiggled her toes.

"How did the filming itself go?"

"Mr. Cecil made us work hard. Not a moment's rest. Aunt Betty plays my dead mother. That's why she was on ice. Uncle Wayne is Dr. Frankenstein, and he wants to bring her back to life. But his first experiment goes all wrong and . . . I shouldn't spoil it."

"A monster chases you, I bet."

"Well, at some point yes. But this is where it gets interesting. We had sound people there. They're not capturing all our words, just getting ready for the scream scene—I mean the Release of the Inner Pain of Life scene. Mr. Cecil had me practice and he played back some of the recordings. It was eerie. All those screaming lessons have paid off. The hairs on the back of my neck are still standing up. To hear your own voice played back to you." She gave Beatrice a pitiful look. "Rub my shoulders. I really need it."

Beatrice did so, gently placing her tanned fingers on her sister's pale skin. She felt as if she were somehow taking the weight from her.

Is the connection between us stronger when I touch her? she wondered.

She sent the message: *Isabelle, say thanks for the massage.* No, that wouldn't be a proper test of their connection; she might say thanks anyway.

Isabelle, mention our parents. Mention Mother and Father.

This was not as common a topic of conversation. They were from so far away and long ago that it was as if they had only existed in fairy-tale land.

Mention them. Tell me you miss them. Mention them.

"Do you think Mother could have been an actress?" Isabelle asked.

Beatrice took her fingers away.

"Don't stop, Beets."

She kept massaging. "Maybe. She was very pretty." The only picture they had of their mother sat on Isabelle's side of the dresser. *The photo could have influenced the question,* Beatrice decided. *I should have asked her to talk about polar bears or airships. Just to eliminate coincidence.*

"All this skill came from somewhere," Isabelle whispered. "Mr. Cecil says it's in my blood and bones. And Mother is where I got the blood and bones from."

Beatrice glanced at the picture of their mother. Beatrice looked nothing like her. Her mother had given everything to Isabelle.

1. My birth killed my mother. Fact.
2. It was not my intention. Fact.
3. If I didn't exist, my mother would be alive. Fact.

Beatrice took her hands away from her sister. "It's time to sleep. You have a big day tomorrow." She stood up and got into bed.

"Don't I know it. There's one more thing I have to tell you, sis."

"What?"

"There's going to be a surprise in this movie. Something in it just for you. Well, it will surprise everyone else who watches it, too. It's going to be amazing." She giggled. "And you're involved."

"What do you mean?"

"Oh, Beets. It's a secret. Mr. Cecil made us all take double-dog-dare vows of secrecy. But it'll knock your socks off."

Beatrice turned out the light, then slid back under the sheets.

"It's funny," Isabelle said. "Seeing Aunt Betty pretending to be dead got me thinking. Do you ever wonder what happens when we die?"

"Our hearts stop beating," Beatrice said. "Blood no longer pumps to the brain. Our thoughts go out one by one."

"Ugh! You're such a spoilsport. I know what heaven is, Beets. It's a place with bright lights and it's full of love and adoration. And you float in all of that for eternity. I'm one hundred percent certain about it."

"That sounds boring."

"No. It sounds heavenly. I'd do anything to get to a heaven like that."

12

August was dead. September was rising up and bringing slightly cooler air. Beatrice stood watching the waves on the endless Pacific Ocean instead of doing her math. The garden where the party had been four days ago was spotless. Lost in thought, she finally turned and went to the opposite window. Santa Monica lay below her, beyond that Los Angeles, and far, far out of her sight were the Hollywood Hills and the Cecil Productions studio. Isabelle was in that studio right now, trying not to let one bead of sweat scar her makeup. Beatrice wished she could see that world through her sister's eyes. *Impossible! We can't seem to share a single thought telepathically unless it involves cream puffs.*

A glint attracted her attention. A small car was coming down the estate road: a police coupe two-seater with a red light on top. The light was not flashing. The coupe turned away from the mansion toward Mr. Cecil's cottage.

She made a gut decision. She carefully opened the door and crept down the spiral stairs and out into the yard. She avoided the main path to Mr. Cecil's and instead followed a trail through bushes and shrubs.

The walls of Mr. Cecil's cottage formed a perfect circle. The windows were more like archery slits and the house itself looked to be constructed from black shadow. Though the place was shadowy, Beatrice admired its simplicity. Mr. Cecil had enough money, he could have built the Tower of London, but instead had chosen this spartan home. He knew how to put on a show, but wasn't ostentatious. Perhaps it came from his modest background. He'd been a poor immigrant from somewhere in Eastern Europe, after all.

She'd observed Mongo bringing many deliveries to this door. Sometimes he'd arrive in a truck and strange, swarthy workmen would help him carry in large wooden boxes. Uncle Wayne had told her the boxes were stuffed with the parts Mr. Cecil needed to create his many cameras and projectors. There had been a particular flurry of packages over the past few months for his Cinétone recorder.

Though Beatrice had watched Mrs. Madge, Uncle Wayne, and Aunt Betty walk into Mr. Cecil's home, he had expressly forbidden her, Isabelle, and any other children from entering. He never gave a reason why.

The officer was standing outside the front door of the cottage, his coupe glinting in the sun behind him. Beatrice stopped and crouched next to a statue of Minerva. The policeman was built in the shape of the letter O: a neckless egg with a head, arms, and legs. His uniform was a dark bruised blue and there was a gun in his leather holster. Beatrice was mostly used to seeing police on the silver screen.

The door opened and Beatrice ducked down farther.

"Thank you for calling ahead, Sergeant Muckler," Mr. Cecil said.

"It's a courtesy, sir." The officer's voice was deep and gravelly. "I know you're a busy man. I just have a few questions."

"I'll do my best to answer them."

"Well, a family has insisted on an investigation into their missing relative. Robert Russel. He's a newspaperman who was last seen at your party."

"I'm sorry to hear that he's missing but the party was only a few days ago. And this is a town where—how shall I put it?—people often disappear into dens of iniquity for weeks at a time."

"Oh, don't I know it, Mr. Cecil," the sergeant said. "This photographer pal of his says he couldn't find Russel, so he went back to the office around ten that night to make some photo-filing deadline. When was the last time you saw Russel?"

"At around eight P.M. I spoke with Mr. Russel along with the other reporters, but I retired from the party early in the evening. He may have found a ride to another celebration. You're welcome to search the grounds."

The sergeant cleared his throat. "Not necessary, sir. He won't be the first to run off with some wannabe starlet."

"No, sadly he won't."

He's not that type, Beatrice wanted to say.

"None of your actors saw him in distress or acting in an odd manner?"

Mr. Cecil crossed his arms. "There was some talk that he overindulged. I don't want to be spreading rumours, though."

"He won't be the first to have done that, either, sir. My theory is he found another party. Then another. He's probably still sauced."

Beatrice peered around Minerva's leg. The sergeant had shifted position so that his face was visible. His nose looked as if it had been broken and reset without any thought to its original shape.

"Well, I do hope he's found," Mr. Cecil said. "For his family's sake."

"No stone shall be left unturned. I just wanted to make you aware of developments and such and let you know that the case has been assigned to me. It's early on in the investigation and these sorts of things can stretch on for, well, years."

"I've always appreciated your discretion, Sergeant Muckler. Especially your sensitive treatment of the pool accident."

"Only doing my job, Mr. Cecil. I'll keep you informed if anything else comes up."

Mr. Cecil drew a grey envelope from his coat and handed it to Sergeant Muckler. The sergeant stuffed the envelope into his trouser pocket. "How is Mrs. Muckler these days?" Mr. Cecil asked.

"She's doing swell, sir, thank you for asking."

"And your children, Jack Junior and Susan?"

"Also swell, sir. I really appreciate your time. I'll take my leave now."

"Wish them my very best, Sergeant."

The officer turned and got into his car and drove away. Beatrice sat perfectly still, leaning against the statue. The goddess's toes poked into her back. She waited a full five minutes but didn't hear the door close. She pulled herself up using Minerva's hand. Her legs had gone to sleep. Mr. Cecil was back inside his house. She made her way along her secret path.

The idea that Robert Russel had disappeared into a den of iniquity was illogical. He was not the type, though he may have imbibed just to get more information for his column. He could've had a heart attack and be lying in some bushes, dead. No, the groundskeepers would have found him by now.

Mr. Cecil had given Sergeant Muckler an envelope. It had to be money. Perhaps some sort of bribe. But Mr. Cecil wasn't the type who needed to bribe anyone. He never broke the law.

She went back up the marble stairs to the top of the tower. She had an *Animalia arthropoda insecta odonata epiprocta anisoptera* waiting in her killing jar: a big red skimmer dragonfly. A particularly handsome catch.

She stopped at the door to her schoolroom. Mr. Cecil was sitting in the wicker chair with his back to her.

"Please come in, Beatrice," he said without turning. "I'd like to talk to you." She walked in and sat at a desk across from him. He was not smiling. "Did you hear anything interesting?"

"When? I was just in the India room drinking tea."

"Please don't lie. It's beneath you. You overheard that the reporter is missing."

"Yes. I did. I . . . I was eavesdropping."

"I'm glad you're not lying to me now. But you did lie to me before."

"I did?" She bit her lower lip. "When?"

"On the night of the party. You said you hadn't spoken to Mr. Russel. But he himself mentioned your discussion on that very same night. He threatened to write an unflattering story about you. He even had a headline: 'The Medusa Twin of Isabelle.'"

"He's not that mean."

Mr. Cecil straightened his tie. "His job is to sell papers. When he wakes up in some brothel, he'll remember his conversation with you."

"He wouldn't be in a brothel!"

"You're young and idealistic. He *will* write a story."

"Wh—what's wrong with that?" she asked. "Don't I deserve to be known? By people. By anyone?"

"Oh, Beatrice. You do. You do. And I . . . I can only guess at what's going on in your head. He's a handsome man. Clever with words. And you. Well, you're good with words, too. Maybe he was able to pry some of those words out of you."

"We just chatted, Mr. Cecil." She crossed her arms. "He wouldn't write a mean story."

"If I had a dime for every time I've heard that from one of my ex-actors, I'd own a hundred studios. You may see him as a friend. Even as a romantic figure."

She found no words to refute his claims. And she couldn't stop from blushing.

He set his hands on his knees. "I'm here to protect you and your sister."

"I don't need protection."

"You do." This was nearly a whisper. "I won't let these people hurt you. It's important that you have no further contact with Robert Russel. I won't make you promise, Beatrice. I just want you to know that I am on your side. Always. I wish I could make you see that."

"Why did you give that policeman money?" she blurted. "Was it a bribe?"

"A bribe?" He recoiled slightly from her words. "Do you think that little of me? You're old enough to know that not everyone walks the straight and narrow. Years ago, Sergeant Muckler fell on hard times. Alcohol. Gambling. His family would sometimes go without food because of his addictions. But I took him under my wing. I helped him to stand up straight. To get a good job as an officer of the law. And I continue to pay his debts."

"Oh," Beatrice said. "That's good of you." It certainly sounded like a plausible answer. Believable, she decided. But it also rang hollow.

"It was the right thing to do." Mr. Cecil stood up and straightened his suit jacket. "I'm always trying to do the right thing. I must return to work. When this film is finished and there's time to relax, I'll take you out hunting for insects, Beatrice."

"You'll take me off the estate?"

"Yes. Soon. Perhaps to Mexico's oyamel fir forest where the monarch butterflies gather."

Her jaw dropped. "That would be amazing." She wasn't certain if she even wanted to hope for such a trip.

"Then we'll make it a reality. You just need to be patient."

He crossed the floor and patted her shoulder. "Isabelle is doing extremely well today. She'll be home late. I do need you to support her. I know you always do, Beatrice." He strode out of the room.

She went back to her insect collection. The dragonfly had been in the chloroform too long and broke into pieces when she tried to pin it.

13

It was the last day of shooting—the day the scream would be recorded forever. All the electric fans would be turned off so their noise wouldn't be picked up by the Cinétone. And because it was a boiling-hot day it meant it would be a double boiler of a day inside the studio under the lights. Beatrice felt some pity for her sister.

Beatrice changed into her maillot swimming suit. The style showed her muscular arms and the skirt only covered halfway down her thighs. Farm-girl legs, that's what Isabelle had called them. Beatrice preferred to think of them as sturdy. She stopped briefly to run her callused hands over her pockmarked skull, then pulled on a swimming cap, grabbed a towel, and trotted down the spiral staircase and out the glass doors to the Neptune pool. It lay exactly between the two wings of the mansion.

She stopped at the pool. This was where Jolly had drowned.

Hypothesis:
Repeatedly facing your fears will erase them.

Proofs:
For the first two years I couldn't swim here. First I
sat in the chair next to the pool. Then months later
I sat on the edge of the pool and dipped my toes in.
And now I can swim without fear.

The memory of Jolly burned more brightly than any other poolside memories from all her years of swimming.

Beatrice had spent the whole day of the one and only Orphan Party watching through her telescope from the tower as the orphans in their white dresses and white slacks and shirts trotted and traipsed around the estate. Many of them walked in pairs, holding hands as they strode up the hill to the Pluto Zoo.

Beatrice found herself staring at the tallest of them all, a girl with one white feather in her headband—it made her look like a young flapper. She was obviously saucy, her hair was bright red, and she had a rash of freckles, the cousin to birthmarks, across her face. At one point she looked up at the tower and waved.

Beatrice had hidden beside the window for several minutes after that. The girl noticed things. Had noticed her! And had waved.

Later, the group had a picnic lunch on the grass, where photographers from several papers took pictures of Isabelle and the orphans. It was all for show, as Isabelle was playing a street urchin in *The Gypsy Ghost* and these snapshots would appear in all the major papers.

At the end of the party they all ate cake with freshly

churned ice cream. Beatrice salivated. Mrs. Madge brought up a piece of cake with ice cream.

The party had ended in the late afternoon and a large red convertible bus came to return the orphans to the Cecil Orphanage for Opportunities building in downtown Los Angeles.

"What was the tallest girl's name?" Beatrice had asked Isabelle as they lay in bed that night.

"Oh, her? Jolly. She was the only one who didn't smell so bad."

Somehow Jolly had not ended up on that vehicle. She'd hidden herself on the estate.

Later in the night a girl's crying had awakened Beatrice. She'd gotten out of bed and stared down at the pool. She could see the glittering water, but couldn't spot the source of the distress. Beatrice dressed and descended the stairs and went out the French doors.

She found Jolly floating face down near the edge of the pool, her feathered hairband stuck to her skull. The roar of the ocean slowly began to fill Beatrice's ears. Nothing else. No thoughts. The closer she got to the body the louder the sound of the ocean became. She reached out and touched the girl's arm and the sound stopped. The flesh was cold. The girl didn't respond.

"Wake up," Beatrice whispered. "Wake up." Jolly did not wake.

Jolly's arms had several unsightly red welts. The girl looked so much like a wet doll that it was hard to believe she'd been walking and crying only a few minutes earlier.

Mongo came around the corner of the mansion and gently lifted Beatrice, then set her down on the chaise longue. He then picked the wet body out of the pool, water dripping from the girl's hair and her white dress. Mongo pointed back to the open door of the mansion and a guttural noise came from that tongueless mouth. The message was clear: he wanted Beatrice to return to bed. Lights were coming on in La Casa Grande. Beatrice slowly climbed the stairs and went to bed in her clothes.

It was such a bright memory she could nearly touch it. Could nearly *go* there.

But she had to forget it. To fight against it every time she came to the Neptune pool. She dropped the towel, dove into the turquoise water, and swam as far as she could under water, surfaced, then did several lengths without stopping. With each stroke she had the sense she was swimming away from something dark.

In time Beatrice climbed out of the pool and lay on a chaise longue in the sun to get rid of the chill that had overtaken her. She leaned back and sighed. The sun had darkened her skin and had also made the birthmarks larger. They are my armour, she told herself.

In scientific language they are called nevus. *The plural being* nevi.

It was easier to think of them as *nevi*. To reduce them to their scientific name. But *birthmark* was also the proper word. For they had marked her since birth.

She had the sensation someone was watching her. All of La Casa Grande's blinds were shut against the afternoon sun and the kitchen had no windows. She opened one eye and squinted at the row of palm trees at the far end of the pool.

A footstep sounded behind her and before she could turn, she was soaking wet.

14

"Raul!" Beatrice leapt to her feet.

Raul was holding a pail. Small chunks of ice had scattered between them. "I took the time to visit the icebox," he explained. "The water didn't feel cold enough." He smiled, showing straight white teeth.

"You'll pay for this!" She grabbed a chunk of ice and threw it hard, but he dodged.

"She who thinks big thoughts is easily snuck up on."

"*Sneaked* is the word." Already the sun was warming her and melting the ice. "Did I mention you'll pay for this?"

"Aw, no harm done. And by the way, that's a nice cap."

"Stop joking. And stop trying to change the subject." She blushed a little and stroked the cap that hid her skull, pausing to play with the flower that adorned the top. She tested the aviator-style strap. "Isabelle picked it out for me. It's made of the finest latex. Very fashionable."

"You make it fashionable."

He gazed at her face for a moment and she wondered if he was staring at her birthmarks. He'd never mentioned them in all the years they'd been playing together. She was torn between punching him and giving him a hug. Instead:

"Let's go for a walk, Raul. I've spent the whole morning inside."

"Are you gonna change out of your swimmer's suit?"

"No. It's too hot. And I might just take a dip in the ocean." She walked in her bare feet, which were callused by years without shoes. She led him past the end of the pool and back toward the garden. They went in silence for some time, the silence that old friends cultivate. Finally, Beatrice asked, "So what are you thinking about?"

"Donkey urine."

"What!"

"That's what I always tell Papá. He asks, 'What are you thinking about, son?' and I say, 'Donkey urine.' Then he doesn't ask again."

"Are you telling me to shove off?"

"No. I'm saying I was thinking about nothing. It's refreshing! You should try it."

Beatrice slapped him on the back, hard enough that he rubbed the spot. They followed the stone walkway on the west side of the property down to the beach. "How many thousands of years have those waves been hitting this coast?" she asked.

Raul shrugged. "Three or four thousand, maybe."

"Oh, much longer than that," she said. "Hundreds of thousands of years. Millions, in fact."

"Well, you've got the great big brain. You'd know." He was staring out at the horizon with a half smile, watching the seagulls in the distance.

"The ocean makes one feel small, doesn't it?" she said.

"No. I just want to swim across it. Or draw it."

"Oh, if you do draw it, I'd love to have that picture."

"Maybe. Maybe not. Let's wait until your birthday and see what happens."

Beatrice gave him an inquisitive look, wondering if he really meant that, but he only stared out at the water.

They continued along the beach, their footprints following them. The sand squished between Beatrice's toes, clung along the top of her foot. She thought briefly about going up to the Pluto Zoo on the hill, but it was so blazingly hot that all the animals would be hiding in their little wooden houses or nests. There was nothing more boring than overheated monkeys and zebras. And they were all so tame—even the lion, who'd appeared in several movies alongside her uncle. They were pale copies of wildlife.

"Let's play hide-and-seek," Raul said.

"We're too old for that."

"It's all in the way you play it. Hide-and-seek and truth-or-dare."

"What? What kind of game is that?"

"One I just made up. You hide first. If I find you then you'll have to answer my truth-or-dare." There was something wolfish and intriguing about his look.

"You'll never ever find me," Beatrice said.

"I always find you. It's easy-peasy."

"Fine." She tugged her bathing cap tighter. "I'll play."

"I'll count to a hundred. You hide. See you in a hundred and three seconds." He made a show of covering his eyes and started counting.

Beatrice ran, her bare feet pounding on the soft grass. Isabelle had once said that truth-or-dare often led to kissing. At least it had once when Ronald, an actor Izzy's age, tried to play it with her (he was fired from the set that very day). Perhaps a kiss was Raul's goal. Her heart beat a little faster. It didn't matter—he wouldn't find her.

She was partway up the hill, passing close to Mr. Cecil's cottage. She knew Raul was frightened of the place, so she guessed it'd be the last area he'd check. She stepped right up to one of the windows, stood on her tiptoes, and grabbed the stone sill. She pulled herself up, crouched on the ledge, and peeked inside.

The study had a large mahogany desk in the centre. A hand-cranked projector sat in the middle of that desk, with two canisters of film leaning against it. Beside that was a phonograph—on second glance she saw that it was attached to the projector with several cables. It was some kind of sound machine, perhaps an early version of the Cinétone. There was a rolling desktop along the wall. Next to it was a tall Egyptian sarcophagus with crossed arms, the only noticeable ornament in the room.

There wasn't any visible proof that Mr. Cecil dined alone in his study. Maybe that took place in a windowless room in the heart of the cottage.

A glass bauble on the desk glowed with electricity. Her fingers itched to touch it. Mr. Cecil would never know.

She pushed, but the window wouldn't open inward. She shoved harder, her muscles burning, and it flicked open, exhaling the air inside.

"What are you doing!"

She turned and nearly fell off. Raul was standing below her, his eyes wide.

"Playing hide-and-seek," she said. "Playing to win."

"You can't go in there."

"I can. I will."

And, without completely intending to, Beatrice stepped down into the study and stood on the hardwood floor, breathing in an overpowering antiseptic smell.

15

The room was silent and cool as if the heat didn't dare enter. Sand had fallen off Beatrice's toes onto the hardwood. She leaned back out the narrow window. Raul stood with his hands on his hips. "You went inside!"

"There's no one here," she said. "Come join me."

"Are you nuts? If I get caught, my father could get fired."

"Mr. Cecil wouldn't do that."

"Says you." He pointed his finger at her.

"C'mon, be brave."

Raul narrowed his eyes. "Brave? What'll your punishment be? No bedtime reading? We'd have to find a new job, a place to live. Even food."

Beatrice bit her lip. Raul was right. He was risking far more than she would ever have to.

In fact, when she looked closely at it, she was hardly risking anything at all. Mr. Cecil had been very clear that neither she nor Izzy should enter his cottage, but he'd never said what the punishment would be. She couldn't picture any punishment that would outweigh the deliciousness of being inside his study and learning his secrets. She should have sneaked in here years ago.

"He wouldn't hurt me," she said. "He thinks of me as his daughter. You can be my lookout."

"Be quick!"

Beatrice went directly to the magic bauble on his desk. Embedded in three upturned talons, it was half the size of her head, swirling with pink and blue electricity. It looked like one of Nikola Tesla's plasma globes. She touched it. The colours danced around her fingers, the hairs on her arms stood up straight. The glass was warm and when she pushed hard on it, it felt as if her hand might sink right into the ball. The longer she stared at the moving colours, the more she felt as if time was slowing and the world was shifting gently into another shape, another form. It took some willpower to pull her hand away.

The projector had slots for several reels, and the words *Morpheus XII* were written on a golden plate attached to its side. Mr. Cecil even named his projectors! The lens was a bulbous honeycomb of glass that looked more like the eye of a giant insect than an electric bulb. Beside it was the Cinétone, a phonograph-like device.

Beatrice gently touched the projector's On switch but paused. She didn't want to spoil any of the story's suspense for herself. After all, Isabelle had said there was a surprise in the movie.

She went to the far wall. Shelves of black books stretched from floor to ceiling, all the silver titles in Latin and Greek. She opened one and stared at the words, wishing she could read Latin. She'd mention that to Mrs. Madge. She flipped to the next page—an ink drawing of a large male body being dissected, the entrails spilling out like snakes. She slammed the book closed and shoved it back on the shelf.

She tiptoed over to the sarcophagus. It was taller than her, and the image of the pharaoh was painted brightly. The Egyptian coffin had been built with much more artistry and workmanship than any of the replicas used in Mr. Cecil's movies. On the very top of it, at a jaunty angle, was a brown fedora that looked as if it had just been tossed up there and forgotten. Maybe there were Egyptian baubles inside. She tugged on the lid, but it was locked. *Bah, there's probably nothing but spiderwebs in there.*

The hat intrigued her. It didn't belong to Mr. Cecil—he always wore white panama hats imported directly from Ecuador. She reached for it, but at that same moment the floorboard creaked behind her. She turned, bringing her arms up in reflex.

Raul was inside the study, one hand on the windowsill, wiping sweat from his forehead.

"Didn't you hear me call?" he whispered. "You've been in here for twenty minutes."

"What? It hasn't even been five minutes."

"No. It's been way too long. Get out."

"Don't be a wet blanket. Mr. Cecil won't be home until late."

"Someone might see the open window."

She walked over and pulled the window shut. "There," she said. The room filled with static electricity as if cutting the room off from the outside world had somehow charged it. The hairs on her arms stood on end again. "Maybe I shouldn't have done that."

There was a low buzzing sound.

"What's that noise?" Raul asked.

Beatrice tilted her head, listening. "It's coming from over there." She went to a nearby cupboard, put her hand on the gold knob, then opened the mahogany door. Inside was a large glass jar, but it was too dark to see why it was buzzing. She brought the jar into the light.

Several hornet-like insects circled inside, wings whirring, mandibles opening and closing. They had long tails with stingers.

"A collection of live scorpion hornets!" Beatrice whispered. "He actually has living specimens."

The size of the nearest insect was magnified by the glass. She inspected the tiger spots along its carapace. Raul came closer and the insects landed on his side of the jar. A jumble of white sticks rested at the bottom.

"Are those bones?" Raul asked.

"From a mouse, judging by the skull. These *Vespidae* actually eat flesh. And look . . ." She pointed at a few larger bones. "Those bones are from a human finger. See the remaining fingernail?"

"Why would there be finger bones?"

Beatrice had no answer to that. Not even a hypothesis.

With a *tick* an insect tapped the glass with its tail as if it were trying to sting her. Another landed beside it and the two tapped at the glass in unison, both of them glaring at her with their compound eyes.

"What are they?" Raul asked. "I've never seen an insect like them."

"I don't know their real names. I call them scorpion hornets because of their tails."

Tick. Tick. Tick. The green venom from their tails dripped down and pooled at the jar's bottom.

Beatrice brought the jar closer to her face, squinting at their buzzing, moving bodies. They were not from this part of the world, she was certain of that.

Beatrice! Help me! Help!

Beatrice blinked and felt unsteady on her feet. Had she heard Izzy's voice? She slowly shook her head, resisting the urge to fall to her knees.

Beatrice! Help!

She turned to Raul. "There's something wrong with Isabelle."

As she spoke, she knew with certainty that Isabelle had experienced a deep pain. Had perhaps fallen and smashed her head. Or her heart had stopped. Beatrice's own heart was pounding.

"How do you know?" he said.

"I just do." She grew weaker and wavered for a moment. Raul caught her by the shoulder but her hands were too cold and clammy to hold on to the jar.

It fell, tumbling over and over.

The jar shattered on the floor. The scorpion hornets stayed in place for a moment, tails curling and uncurling, then they flapped the glass dust off their wings and rose into the air.

16

Raul grabbed Beatrice's hand and pulled her toward the door to the hallway. A scorpion hornet buzzed past her head, its wings brushing her earlobe. She jerked out of the way, slapping at the air.

"Ahhh!" Raul collapsed as if he'd been shot. Beatrice bent down and smacked a hornet off his neck, the back of her hand burning where the venom spattered her skin. Another scorpion hornet darted straight at her eyes. She batted it away, then bent down and tried to lift Raul, but he was too heavy. Instead she had to dig in her heels and drag him toward the door.

"I. Can. Walk," Raul said. He pulled himself to his feet.

The hornets arrayed themselves in a semicircle and blocked the path to the door. *It's like they can think.* They hovered in the air, flicking their tails. Venom dripped, burning tiny holes in the floor.

"The window," Beatrice huffed, but the moment she took a step in that direction three of the hornets broke out of the semicircle and blocked the way to the window.

"They're anticipating our actions," she whispered.

"Then let's do something they can't anticipate." Raul's

hand covered the growing welt on his neck, but a bit of blood and pus leaked between his fingers. "What if we just stand still?"

"You're going to pass out at any moment." She glanced around the room. "Maybe they'll react to this."

She flipped a switch on the projector and that odd bulb sent light to a small screen. Several of the hornets darted straight toward it, leaving an open path to the hallway door.

"Run!" Beatrice pushed Raul out of the room, tumbled after him, then slammed the door. Two of the scorpion hornets smacked into the door's window, buzzing angrily, their tails twitching and spattering the glass with green venom.

"Did any of them make it through?" Raul asked. His breath was ragged.

"No. I don't think—" A scorpion hornet buzzed right past her nose. She swung, but the thing dove, looped downward and landed on her bare leg. She slowly lifted her hand. Her heart thudded. Once. Twice.

The insect stared up at her. Its tail arced down. It was like being stabbed with a burning-hot needle. She collapsed as the scorpion hornet darted off. It took all her strength to stand. She swatted madly as the insect flew around her head again. Raul windmilled his arms too, and the two of them began to work their way down a long hall, the scorpion hornet in pursuit.

She yanked a painting from the wall and swung it, knocking the insect out of the air. The thing thudded to the ground. Raul jumped on it before the hornet could right itself. It took two hard stomps before its carapace snapped open and its insides spattered across the floor. Smoke came up from the hardwood. The sole of his shoe was smoking, too. He jumped back as the broken scorpion hornet jittered and snapped its tail, trying to strike them. Beatrice stumbled over to a podium, lifted the marble head of Jupiter into the air and smashed it into the creature.

Then they retreated to the end of the hall, charged through the door they found there, and tumbled outside into Mr. Cecil's private garden. Beatrice slammed the door closed, and the two of them kept running.

17

Raul and Beatrice didn't stop until they were well away from the cottage and hidden by several orange trees. The buzzing of bees and other insects was alarming. Beatrice leaned against a tree for support.

"Your neck needs to be drained," she said. A raw, red lump the size of a croquet ball had sprouted inches from his Adam's apple. Raul scratched the flesh, making more pus leak out. "Don't rub it!"

"It itches!" He grabbed his right hand with his left and held it against his chest.

"Believe me, I know." She let out a long breath. "We don't want to get blamed for all that mess."

"We broke a jar, smashed a painting, and knocked over a god's head. We're going to get blamed."

"No. No. We have to pretend we weren't even together today. No one saw us. I was busy reading and you . . . you were off trimming vines. Mr. Cecil might think it was thieves. Like the ones who robbed the zoo last year."

"Maybe . . . maybe he'll think that." Raul didn't sound like he believed his own words. "We can't just leave those insects flying around in there."

"Mr. Cecil must know how to deal with them. And it's not like we can go back inside. Jeez, that lump is getting bigger." Raul's white shirt was now stained by sweat and drops of blood and pus. "You'll have to hide that from your dad. From everyone. Or Mr. Cecil will know it was us. At least I was smart enough to be stung on the leg."

"Yes, you're so brainy. I'll wear a scarf. Do you have any extra ones?"

"Oh, ha. A neckerchief will do, of course. And you should get some antiseptic on it."

"We have gallons of antiseptic," Raul said. "Gardeners get used to insect bites. And a neckerchief will make me look like a cowboy. Mexicans are the real cowboys." His tone was light, but there was strain in his face.

"I'm sorry I got you into this, Raul."

"I am, too. Sometimes I let you get under my skin too much." He shrugged, then winced at the movement. "I didn't have to climb up there. But I wanted to. You were seeing things that I really did want to see."

They walked to the front door of his cottage. "Can you make it back to the house on your own?" he asked.

She nodded. And then she didn't know what came over her—maybe she wanted to thank him properly: she kissed him on the cheek. Perhaps she did it because they had been so close to action, possibly to death if they'd been bitten enough times. Or maybe the venom was driving her mad, making her brain think crazy things and making her body do them. For a moment she no longer felt her leg. Only his warm cheek.

He blushed. She laughed. "You look like you're going to hell in a handbasket, Raul."

"It's the latest style." He leaned against the cottage's stucco wall. "Thanks for the adventure, friendbird." He opened the door and turned back to say, "I hope your sister isn't hurt."

"I hope so, too." With that, Beatrice limped along her secret paths. Her body was arctic cold, her whole leg a frozen chunk of meat. Then her flesh became so hot she thought she'd melt. Every pore dripped sweat. She crossed the closely cropped grass, cut by Raul's father and the other brown-skinned men. She forced herself through the Pomona garden, up the stone stairs one at a time, and finally, she shoved open the French doors. The long spiral staircase inside the west wing felt as high as Everest.

She hobbled to the washroom and pawed the toiletries out of the cupboard, letting them fall on the floor, until she found the tin medical kit. Then she sat down, the cold of the toilet seat shocking her bare legs. She opened the kit and found gauze, scissors, and a glass bottle of Sparkers Antiseptic.

Beatrice's eyes were blurring. Each beat of her heart made the sting throb. She looked at her leg. A tangerine-sized lump had formed on the side of her calf (with a jagged hole in the middle). Pale green pus was already leaking out.

The longer she stared, the more familiar the lump appeared. She had, of course, recently seen one on Raul's neck. But she had seen something like it before that, too. She had categorized so many bug bites in her notebooks, mostly from first-hand experience. But she could not place where she'd seen this type before.

Beatrice lifted the empty red Mavis Talcum tin and pulled off the lid. She reached for a pair of tweezers. A stinger stuck out of the wound. It looked like a long, sharp grey serrated needle. She tried twice to squeeze it with the tweezers, but failed. On the third try she was pretty certain she had a good grip. She pulled. It was as if she were fish-hooking a whole pound of flesh from her leg. Beatrice grunted with the exertion. She didn't want to faint; it was what the delicate women did in the British novels she read—passing out at the sight of blood or a sudden shock of fear. She'd always yell *Get up!* at the book—at them—whenever that happened.

Darkness blossomed in the centre of her vision but she continued to pull. Then, with a last tug, the stinger came free. It was about an inch long and the thickness of a bobby pin. Sharp barbs poked out all along its sides. It curled and flexed as if it were still alive. She tossed the stinger into the tin can. *Thunk*. She screwed the lid tight.

The stinger started banging against the side of the can as she set it down.

Beatrice grabbed the bottle of Sparkers Antiseptic. Just seeing the dark orange liquid sloshing inside the brown bottle made her grit her teeth. Mrs. Madge had applied this burning antidote several times throughout Beatrice's childhood, usually when she'd had rather bad scrapes from crashing her bicycle on the driveway. It was like pouring acid on a wound.

Beatrice dumped a healthy amount of the Sparkers onto a white face cloth, staining it orange, and held it against the sting. It took all her strength not to scream. When she pulled away the cloth, the pain slowly subsided. She began to pour the Sparkers directly into the festering sore, clamping her teeth together. She grew dizzier. Now her whole leg was burning, as if the lump were fighting the antiseptic.

She wiped up the wound as well as she could. The moment she stood, the pressure on her leg sent a pain shooting through it. Despite that, she put the bathroom back in order. No point having Mrs. Madge snoop around here. She'd report anything she observed directly to Mr. Cecil.

She carried the antiseptic-stained face cloths back to her room in one hand, the can in the other. The stinger continued to rattle.

Why is it doing that?

It had to be a dying electrical signal. The stinger couldn't still be alive. It would wither on its own. Maybe her blood was somehow keeping it alive. An ant's legs would still move for a while if you pulled off its head.

She took the can and stained cloths and stuffed them under a pile of clothes in the back of the closet, then set Gibbon's *The History of the Decline and Fall of the Roman Empire* on top of them all. She closed the closet door.

She glimpsed herself in the full-length mirror. She was pale and stupid looking—stupid because she was still in her bathing suit, the bathing cap on her head. As if she'd been out for a jaunty swim. Her birthmarks stood out; her legs were alabaster white, as if the blood had been drained from them. She carefully changed from her bathing suit into her khaki trousers and shirt. As she was pulling a scarf tightly around her head she heard, through the open window, the clunking of the front gates.

Beatrice went to the window. The gates stood open, as though allowing passage of an invisible car. The nose of the Lincoln Town Car appeared in the far driveway. It approached the road that wound its way up the hill to the mansion, moving slowly, as though leading a funeral procession.

Isabelle was coming home.

18

Beatrice lurched to the stairwell. Each movement felt as if she were stepping on a land mine. There were seventy steps in total. At the bottom she stumbled awkwardly across the foyer's marble floor. She shoved open the front doors of La Casa Grande and swayed into the bright light, shading her eyes with her hand.

The Lincoln Town Car rolled silently along the road and came to a stop on the brick driveway. Mongo stepped out and lumbered around to the passenger side of the car. He looked down from his mountaintop head and his eyes met Beatrice's. Perhaps there was a gentleness in his scarred face. Then he opened the car door and Uncle Wayne stumbled out, his face pale and dotted with perspiration, the smell of sweat and whisky clouding around him. He'd clearly been helping himself to the selection of hard liquor in the Town Car.

"What happened?" Beatrice rasped.

"Shh," Uncle Wayne hushed her. He reached back into the vehicle. When he turned again he was carrying Isabelle. Her white dress was draped over his arms, her skin as pale as her gown, her body limp.

Aunt Betty wobbled out of the car and dabbed at Isabelle's forehead with a handkerchief.

"Izzy!" Beatrice reached out and touched the side of her sister's neck. Isabelle's eyes fluttered open long enough to reveal that they were only white, as though her pupils and irises had faded away.

"She got all fainty on-set," Uncle Wayne said. "She just needs rest, so I'm taking her up to her room. Mr. Cecil promised she'll be fine."

He stepped around Beatrice and carried Isabelle through the mansion's double doors. The train of Isabelle's dress dragged along behind Uncle Wayne as he ascended the spiral staircase. Beatrice and Aunt Betty followed. Aunt Betty stopped on the tenth step, holding her chest and breathing heavy. "I can't go no farther. It's been a horrendously hard day."

Beatrice pushed past her and made it to the bedroom door in time to see Uncle Wayne gently lay Isabelle on the bed.

"I need to know exactly what happened," Beatrice said.

Uncle Wayne brushed at the slick hair on his forehead. "It was the oddest, most amazing thing. She . . . she became Rosella."

"She became who?"

"Rosella. Rosella Frankenstein. It happens to actors sometimes, you wouldn't know about that—you don't do our work. They . . . we . . . well, we act so convincingly that we believe—we believe we've become the character we're playing and that everything around us is real. That's what happened to Izzy. She *became* Frankenstein's daughter."

Beatrice clutched her sister's hand. Her fingers were five icicles. "The fire needs to be lit!" she said.

"We need flames!" Uncle Wayne shouted as if he were on-set and there were invisible set dressers within earshot. "Now!"

Beatrice limped over to the fireplace and lit the gas. Blue-green flames came to life behind the ceramic radiating element. "What knocked her out?" she asked when she returned to the bed. "Did she bump her head?"

"From the moment the final scene started, Isabelle had a scared-rabbit look in her eyes. She ran down the stairs, just as she was supposed to—she hit all her marks. Her timing was perfect. Her nervous glances over her shoulder, the grimace when the rats ran across her bare feet—the cameras captured it all. Then she was cornered in the dungeon and she turned and saw the monster."

"There was a monster?"

Uncle Wayne rubbed at his jaw. "Well, that's the thing. Usually on-set it's just rubber and fake googly eyes and, well, the monsters can look somewhat ridiculous. Mr. Cecil fixes it so they're truly scary in the film. But today no one was chasing her. Mr. Cecil wanted the horror to play out in her imagination. And when Isabelle turned—and the look over the shoulder was so perfect, her face so pale, her mouth opening to scream—she clearly believed something awful was there. She saw it for real! She had become her character."

"But what knocked her out?"

"She screamed herself unconscious. What a scream! The

hairs on the back of my neck stood on end. Everyone shivered, from the cameramen to the gaffers and the best boy. Even the set shook, I swear. It was horrible to hear. It hurt the ears. She so completely believed in whatever it was that she was seeing. The 'scenic truth' that Mr. Cecil always talks about. It was all captured on his Cinétone recorder. Then she collapsed. We just stood there watching until Mr. Cecil said, 'Cut.' Marge went up to congratulate Izzy and maybe apply more greasepaint, but Isabelle wouldn't wake up. Not even smelling salts worked. So Mr. Cecil told me to bring her home. He said she wouldn't need a doctor. He promised she'd be fine." He paused. "And I believe him."

Beatrice put her hand on her sister's cold forehead. The gas fireplace was just beginning to heat the room. "But why isn't she waking up?"

"Exhaustion. That's what Mr. Cecil said. She doesn't need a doctor."

"Stop repeating things!"

He wiped away slaver that had gathered on his lower lip." She gave everything today. It really was a wonderful performance. She'll win awards, I bet. The film is a home run."

"Where's Mr. Cecil? He should be here."

"He has work to do. This was the last scene. Everything else in the movie has been shot. We're done!"

"You mean her screaming was the end of the movie?"

"No. No. Beatrice." He chuckled. "You don't know much about the business, do you? Too much time killing bugs, I guess." He ran his hand through his hair again. "We shot the final scene days ago. It was the big scream scene that we saved for last."

"Is she alive in the final scene?" Beatrice asked. "The scene you already shot."

Wayne was flummoxed for several seconds by the question. "Yes, yes, of course. It's a family reunion. I don't live through to the final scene—Dr. Frankenstein, I should say, doesn't. He gets torn in two and thrown off the highest tower. It's all shown in shadows, of course. You don't want to shock the audience too much. I argued with Mr. Cecil about my death. I really felt the father should defeat the monster. But Mr. Cecil said the caretakers have to die to make the protagonist more vulnerable. It's some rule of storytelling."

"Then who does she reunite with?" Beatrice asked. "You said it was a family reunion."

"It's her mother's twin sister. That's the twist. Her aunt gets out of the hospital. It's the first time the sun appears in the movie. Right at the end it rises and they look up at it, their skin lit by the sun. It's symbolic."

Beatrice grabbed a pillow and held it tightly. "But Isabelle's character survives, right?"

"Yes! Yes. I said that. She survives."

"Well, that's something at least."

"Why?" Uncle Wayne asked.

"Because if she still believes she's Rosella then maybe she'll actually wake up for the happy ending."

19

One hour ticked by on the clock. Then two. Then three. The sun continued to shine on the estate and through the windows of the mansion.

Shortly after the sun set, the bedroom door opened.

"I brought you beef-dumpling stew," Mrs. Madge said, holding a tray containing a large bowl and a glass of milk. Her grey-streaked hair was, as always, tied in a bun.

"Oh," Beatrice said from her position next to Isabelle. "That's nice of you. I don't know if I can eat."

"The stew will give you strength." Mrs. Madge set the tray on the bedside table. "You must be worried about Isabelle. She will get better."

"Can you promise that?" Beatrice asked.

Mrs. Madge shook her head. "No. I've made too many promises in my life. But you sisters are good at bouncing back. Drink up the milk at the very least. It'll settle your stomach."

Beatrice lifted the glass, her hand shaking slightly, and drank half the milk. "Is Mr. Cecil back from the studio?"

"He returned a few hours ago."

"He did?" She hadn't heard his car. It occurred to her that if he'd been stung by the hornets, Mrs. Madge would be treating him right now. So he *did* know how to control them, Beatrice thought.

"Will he be coming to see us?"

"He never mentioned it." Mrs. Madge crossed her arms. "Don't worry about your classes tomorrow. Just rest. Both of you. Now, eat up, child."

She left the room. Steam was still rising off the dumplings and carrots, along with a peppery scent. Beatrice took several mouthfuls, but was only able to finish half the bowl. It did make her feel warm inside. She wished she could somehow transfer that warmth to her sister.

With the food in her stomach, the itching and sharp pain in her leg felt a little duller. She wondered if it was because the blood was going to her intestines now. She leaned back.

She tried to read, but it was too hard to focus on the black letters on a white page. Her eyes would stray and she'd find herself staring at Izzy, wanting her to stir.

Once, when they were eight years old, Beatrice had caught influenza. It was not the Spanish flu that had taken so many lives a few years earlier, but it had been a particularly vicious strain. It had shut her body down, made every muscle ache. Beatrice could hardly lift her head. Mr. Cecil had acted as her doctor, as he had for any other illness. But at night, when the chills were the worst, she would feel Isabelle hug her close and warm her with her own body heat. There was no way to prove that had saved her, but she believed it must have affected the outcome.

The moon stared through the window. Time had passed in the blink of an eye. The gas fireplace was so hot that

Beatrice began to sweat, but still Isabelle remained chilled.

I'm frightened.

Beatrice held completely still. Isabelle's voice had spoken in her head. But her sister hadn't moved or made a sound.

Frightened. Of the face. Don't leave me. DON'T! LEAVE! ME!

She touched Isabelle's shoulder. "*I won't. I won't. I won't,*" Beatrice whispered. She waited. There was no reply.

Beatrice's leg continued to throb. She moved the sheets to the side and looked at the bandage. It was stained yellow. If she touched the skin nearby it sent pain radiating toward the center of the wound.

There was a quick knock and the bedroom door opened. Beatrice threw the sheets back over her leg.

"Hey, Beets!" Uncle Wayne came into the room, his shirt untucked, his chin shadowed by stubble. She was struck by a memory of being much younger and of him giving her whisker rubs and her squealing with laughter. "We've come to check up on the patient."

Aunt Betty followed a heartbeat later, her step that half-lurch that indicated she'd been at the wine again. "How is the patient, Beetsy Weetsy?"

Beatrice bit back a retort and said, "Still sick."

"Oh, Beets," Uncle Wayne said. "You look so worried. She's a strong girl. You've both got your father's blood in your veins. Nothing would kill that old coot."

But he died, Beatrice wanted to shout. *He died in a fire.*

Aunt Betty placed her palm on Isabelle's forehead. "She's cold. Are you sure she's . . . you know . . . she's alive?"

"She's alive!" Beatrice hissed.

Aunt Betty backed up a step. "I didn't mean it that way. Is she warm enough? That's what I meant, Beetsy Weetsy."

"Don't call me that."

"It's just a nickname." Aunt Betty gave a red-eyed blink and spoke slowly and carefully, "And don't you talk to me like that. You show me respect. I'm a grown-up. I raised you. I didn't want to, but I did. I could've had a different life."

"How much have you had to drink?" Beatrice asked.

Aunt Betty lifted a hand as if she were winding up for a slap.

Uncle Wayne stepped between them. "Stop it!" He grabbed Aunt Betty's hand and kissed it dramatically. "You two are so headstrong." He lowered Aunt Betty's hand, but still held on to it. "Mr. Cecil says it's just a growth spurt."

"When did you talk to him?"

"He needed my help with the editing. And he needed to eat."

"You dined with him?"

"No, I never dine with him. No one dines with him. Anyway, he figures Izzy has grown a lot in the last six months. We're changing the marks on the set—the angles for our shots. The cameraman noticed first. Remember when we had to have her stand on a box for most of her films? Not anymore. She's a young woman." He rubbed his chin. "All this work has tired her out and so has the growth spurt. And she hasn't had anything to eat on the set. Maybe a slice of pear and a cracker. She needs her rest. That's what Mr. Cecil says."

"He nearly worked her to death," Beatrice said. "Maybe she's just his meal ticket."

"Don't say that, Beets," Uncle Wayne said. He sniffed in a breath of air, wheezed a bit, and reached out to touch her shoulder. His palms were sweaty. "I know you're upset. But we owe him for everything. These walls around us. My career. Izzy becoming the biggest star in the whole wide world. And me becoming big, too. Really big. And Betty, too. All of us. Big. So don't speak about him like that." He tightened his hand on her shoulder, his fingers digging into her flesh. She tried to shrug his grip off.

Uncle Wayne patted her head with his other hand but kept a tight grip on her shoulder. "You're a smart one, Beets. You've got that going for you. We just came here to tell you that we're heading into town for a late lunch."

"It's nine at night. That's a very late lunch."

"It's fashionably late," Betty said. "We're meeting up with my publicist. She's a bit of a lush. But fun!"

"Is there anything you need?" Uncle Wayne asked. "Spritzer water? Soda pop? A plate of french fries?"

Beatrice shook her head. If she opened her mouth she'd scream.

"You're a good sister." Uncle Wayne took his hands away, and started to tuck his shirt in. She resisted the urge to wipe her shoulder. "Izzy's lucky to have you. *We're* lucky to have you. You're all grown-up."

They left, their footsteps and their voices echoing as they stumbled down the hallway and along the spiral staircase. The front doors opened, and then Uncle Wayne's loud, raucous laughter and Aunt Betty's high-pitched giggle were cut off as the doors closed.

Wayne and Aunt Betty's room was in the east wing of the mansion. They'd never stayed that close to the girls' room, preferring to let the servants comfort the children when they had nightmares. *We're playthings to them.* It wasn't the first time Beatrice had had that thought. *Toys to be taken out when they were in the mood to pretend to be Mother and Father. But when something bad happens, they're off for a late lunch.*

Mr. Cecil was the closest thing they had to a real parent. Though he'd never said *I love you,* he had shown it in the ways he'd patiently dealt with them. He'd taught her so many scientific principles and had always been willing to talk about intellectual things.

But he was willing to work Isabelle to the bone for his stupid movies! She let that thought burn for a moment.

She wondered if word had already gotten out to the press about Isabelle fainting on-set. If so, it would be in the papers tomorrow. Robert Russel would write something clever about it. *No:* she corrected herself. He wouldn't write about it. He hadn't shown up since the party. Maybe he'd moved to Mexico and was trying to write another novel. Or back to Paris.

She lifted a book from her bedside table. "I'm going to read one of your favourites, Isabelle," she said. "It's *The Wizard of Oz.*"

She read aloud, each word falling from her lips. The sound of her own voice helped her focus on the story. How she wished a cyclone would pick up their room and carry them away. Maybe the wizard in Oz could fix all of their problems.

"'Dorothy lived in the midst of the great Kansas prairies,'" Beatrice read, "'with Uncle Henry, who was a farmer, and Aunt Em, who was the farmer's wife. Their house was small, for the lumber to build it had to be carried by wagon many miles—'"

A creaking noise interrupted her.

It came again. *Creak.* Followed by *scrape.* She immediately looked to the door, expecting Mr. Cecil to swing it open. *He's here.* But the door remained closed.

There was a movement in the corner of her vision. A shadow was an inch away from the windowpane. Another persistent knock followed. A hand wiped the fogged glass and a face became clear.

20

Raul. Grinning like mad and waving just as madly.

Beatrice got out of bed, limped over, and unlatched the window. "What are you doing here?" she asked.

He was clinging to the lattice, moonlight making the sweat on his forehead glisten. "I needed to check up on you. To see you."

"I'm fine."

"Cook Zhen said you and Isabelle were on your death-beds. Because you're twins. The grounds staff were taking bets you'd both die before sunrise. The guards, too."

"Bets? But I'm not sick. And neither of us is going to die!"

"I see that. It was gossip—that's what the help does—we natter on about you *important* people."

"I'm not important!"

"Yes," he said, "you are." He was wearing a red necker-chief. A white bandage, stained with a smattering of orange and bits of red, was peeking over the cloth.

"What if you got caught climbing up to my room?"

"I'm trimming the vine." He held up a strand of Virginia creeper and then dropped it on the windowsill.

"Besides, Mr. Cecil is in his cottage. And Humpty and Dumpty have gone to town." Raul thrust his hand toward her. "Pull me in."

She did so. The hours of helping his father with the cutting and digging were written on his callused hands.

"How's your sting?" she asked.

"My head should fall off any moment now."

"At least you still have your sense of humour." Beatrice went to punch him in the shoulder, but instead gave it a gentle squeeze. Then she limped back to her sister's side. "What would you have done if I was on my deathbed?" she asked once she was settled.

"I'd tell you jokes until you fell off your deathbed." He strode up to her side of the bed.

"Ha! You're a good boy, Raul."

"I'm not a boy!"

"You're right, you're a crazy young wild man. And you scaled the wall like . . . like a gecko."

"A gecko. Thanks." He stuck out his tongue.

"Well, more like a Romeo, then."

"Romeo who?"

"He's from a Shakespeare play. The story ends badly, but most of his plays do. What I mean to say is, thank you, Raul."

"You're welcome, friendbird." He scratched at his bandage. Stopped himself. "And how is your sting?"

"Peachy! My leg should fall off any moment now."

He lowered himself down on the bed a few inches from her feet. "We're stupid, aren't we?"

"No. *I* was stupid. I should've listened to you."

"I *am* amazingly wise. I'm glad you recognize that now."

"Let's not go too far."

Raul pointed his thumb at her sister. "Is Izzy doing all right?"

"I've never seen her like this. I can't feel her."

"What do you mean?"

"Usually, I know exactly where she is. When she enters a room; when she wakes up. I just know she's *there*. But I can't find her now. She's right in the room and I can't find her. Mr. Cecil worked her too hard. The film was more important to him than she was."

"But she was just pretending to be someone. That doesn't sound so hard."

"It's more than that. Acting is . . . well, it's using your energy to become someone else. The film took too much of that energy. And—"

Her sister moved her arm the slightest bit and Beatrice felt a shock of joy. Then, a microsecond later, a sharp fear.

"Get under the bed," she whispered.

"What's wrong?"

There was a *creak* outside the door. The softest of footsteps. "Get under the bed! Now!"

Raul dropped down to the floor the exact moment the door opened. She hoped the ruffle was low enough to hide him.

Beatrice lifted her book up, feigning surprise. But could she really fool a man with such a keen sense of both the real and the pretend?

Mr. Cecil stepped into the room. He was wearing a tan suit, and his greying hair was a little tousled, as if he'd just run his hand through it. "Good evening, Beatrice," he said. "I'm much later than I intended to be."

He approached the bed. He did look concerned. Patches of tiredness lingered below his eyes. As far as she could tell he hadn't been stung by a scorpion hornet. "How is Isabelle?"

"She's sick," Beatrice answered. "You worked her too hard."

"She isn't sick. She fell into herself. It was a wonderful piece of acting—she is such a once-in-a-generation natural. And it was more than that. I—we captured her scream on the Cinétone. The perfect frequency. It will change things."

"What do you mean?" Beatrice set *The Wizard of Oz* down.

"When people watch the film they'll hear that scream and history will spin on its axis. No film will be the same after this. I may even be so bold as to say nothing on earth will be the same." He rested his hand on Isabelle's forehead. "She'll recover. You're right, though. I overtaxed her. But I only ever do what's necessary."

"Was it necessary for her to collapse?"

"The film had to be completed. And Isabelle wanted to give it her all. She said as much to me right before the fainting spell." He clapped his hands together. "I didn't come just to play the physician, I also came as a friendly inquisitor. I have a few questions for you, Beatrice."

"Questions for me?" She had rehearsed her answer: *I was in the tower all day.*

"Yes, young Miss Plato. But you weren't being Socratic today, were you? Instead you were a *girl of action*. The first question I have is: Who were you talking to a moment ago?"

"I—I was reading aloud." She tapped the book. "It makes Isabelle feel better."

"I distinctly heard two voices."

Mr. Cecil came around to her side of the bed but showed no sign he'd seen anyone. He was rubbing the space on his left hand where his little finger had been.

"Why is the window open?" he asked. A gentle question.

"Uh, I was warm. And Isabelle was sweating. We needed fresh air."

He sniffed ever so slightly. "I'm quite certain that boy was here. Did he crawl in the window?"

"No, he's not here," she said. "He hasn't been here. I only spend time with Raul outside."

"Not true. He's been in the house many times. To watch movies. To sneak up to your schoolroom and stare at insects." He sniffed again. "There is the slightest scent of boyish childish desperation in the air. Perhaps he's recently departed. At this very moment he might be standing in the garden looking up. Wanting to love and protect you. I know you're wondering: Will my prince come and rescue me? A hundred thousand girls are thinking that tonight and a hundred thousand boys are wanting to climb a mountain, a tree house, a rope ladder, a"—he paused—"a lattice." He strode over and picked up the strand of Virginia creeper, then looked out the window. "Ah, no sign of any prince. Perhaps the lion has lost his bravery. Like a tin man without a heart."

There was a knocking beneath the bed. Mr. Cecil turned and Beatrice sat up, bumping her head against the headboard.

"He's not outside," she said. "He's never ever been in my room."

Mr. Cecil went to the scorpion hornet on the wall. "The compound eye captures one image, not thousands," he said. "And it's adept at tracking motion."

"I know that," Beatrice said, somewhat defiantly. "But a dead insect sees nothing."

"Don't be so certain about that." He touched the display glass near the insect's head and held two fingers there. After a moment, he nodded. "The boy came in the window. He stood by your bed."

"How can you know that? He—didn't. He's at home."

Mr. Cecil turned away from the hanging insect and rubbed that fingerless space on his left hand again. He strode over to her bedside. His lips were a tight line. "You lied to me about him, Beatrice. And, not so long ago, you lied about Robert Russel. That pattern disappoints me. Our relationship has always been about trust. I've presented all the right traits and have worked so hard to insert myself as a father figure."

"But you are. You are."

He sat lightly on the edge of the bed. "Someone broke into my cottage."

"R-really? Was it robbers?"

"It was an inside job, so to speak. And if you know who it was, then tell me now. I'll forgive your trespasses. You'll rebuild the bridge of trust. Was it that boy?"

"Raul wouldn't go in there."

"Was it you?" He spoke with such gentleness.

A moment passed. Another. It would be so easy just to say yes. To be done with it. But what about Raul? "I—I didn't go in your house. I know I'm not supposed to. I promise it's true."

"A promise is a contract, Beatrice." Mr. Cecil closed his eyes as if he were meditating. He stayed that way for several moments, then opened them slowly. "Our contract has been broken," he said. Then he moved aside the sheet, uncovering her wounded leg. "Your lies are revealed."

"But Mr. Cecil, I—"

He clamped a hand on her knee, tore off the bandage, and thrust his finger directly into the giant welt. "You trespassed in my home," he said very quietly as Beatrice twisted and turned, trying to pull her leg away. "You crossed into my sacred ground—a place designed only for me. But the *Zebûb* has stung you. That's your first taste of the inevitable future."

"You're hurting me! Stop!"

Mr. Cecil stared directly into her eyes and continued to press harder. She arched her back, let out a moan of pain. He didn't stop staring. "Tell me what you saw, Beatrice. And tell me exactly what you did."

"I—I. Ahh. I p-pushed the window open."

"Yes, and you went in. I concluded that. But what did you see? What did you touch? What did you discover?"

"I . . ." Tears were leaking from her eyes. "I didn't see anything. N-nothing. Ahh."

"No more lies."

"Ahh. I—I touched—I touched the bauble thing. And I looked in a book. It had drawings, h-horrible drawings."

"Not for children to see. You are a child. What else? Speak, Beatrice." He jabbed the wound with each word.

"Ahhhh."

"I said speak. Speak the truth, Beatrice Thorn."

"I—I heard...buzzing. I picked up the jar and it slipped."

"And you fled?"

"Yes. *AH.* Yes." Spittle dripped from her lips. "Yes. I f-fled. Stop it. Stop it, please. Mr. Cecil. You're killing me."

His eyes did not waver. "Were you alone?"

She snapped her teeth together hard enough to make a *click. "Ahhh, it hurts so."*

"It's meant to hurt, Beatrice. Pain teaches. The body remembers. The human mind sharpens. Now, answer me. Were you alone?"

Her lips began to move. *Raul. Raul. Raul,* she thought. But she said, *"I—I. Was. By. Myself."*

Mr. Cecil pulled away his finger. He wiped it on the sheets, then gently covered her leg. He patted her shoulder. "I do this only to teach you, Beatrice. I will punish you much more severely if you disobey me again." He stood. "I have my work to do. Keep your vigil with Isabelle and comfort her when she awakes. That is an order." He left the room and closed the door behind him.

It was a full five minutes before Beatrice whispered hoarsely, "He's gone. You can come out now."

Raul pulled himself out from under the bed and climbed

to his feet. He looked pale and smaller. His hands trembled. Beatrice was surprised at her own anger. *Why didn't you save me?* she wanted to shout. But she bit back her words.

"What a bastard," Raul said.

She nearly laughed.

21

The night passed.

Beatrice did not sleep much more than a few minutes at a time. Isabelle still slept soundly. The rising and falling of her chest was almost imperceptible.

Wake up, Isabelle. Wake up. Beatrice tried to send that thought right into her sister's head. *Open your eyes.* But Izzy did not stir.

When the morning light was bright enough, Beatrice pulled back the blankets to see the swelling from the sting had slightly receded. It still throbbed, though. *He laid his hand on me!* Not once in her life could she remember Mr. Cecil ever getting angry. Not once had he raised his voice. And even last night he had spoken with quiet certainty. But he had caused her horrible pain on purpose.

No. With a purpose, she decided. *To control me.*

To put me in my place.

She poked at the flesh around the wound. The welt from the sting was much larger than those she'd had from other insect bites. But it was familiar, too, and it took her a moment to run through her memories of other bites she'd seen. On her own arms. Even on Isabelle's. But the ones that she remembered now were those on Jolly's arms.

Beatrice forced herself to picture Jolly's dead body in the pool. Jolly was floating because there was still air in her lungs. She'd also been wearing a silk dress that would have trapped air (Beatrice knew it was silk because Mr. Cecil had given all the girl orphans silk dresses for the party). Jolly had been making mournful, frightened cries only a minute or so before her death. So what had killed her? Not drowning, obviously.

The large welts had been the only obvious injury. There were at least six of them, if her memory could be trusted (and Beatrice knew memory could not always be trusted) and they were just like her own sting. But judging by the pain that one sting had caused, six would be enough to make you pass out. Or cause you to throw yourself into the pool to try to escape the agony. Then the venom had stopped the orphan's heart.

So Jolly had encountered the same scorpion hornets. And she had died. Perhaps she also sneaked into the cottage. It was curious how that made Beatrice feel as if they were friends. *But what did she discover? And were the hornets let out of their jar on purpose? Perhaps to silence Jolly forever.*

She thought back to the money Mr. Cecil had given the sergeant. Maybe the cop knew the death wasn't an accident, and he had taken the payment to cover up the facts.

Beatrice wondered if the scorpion hornets had bitten anyone else, but Raul had never encountered them before. She also spent time outside nearly every day and actually pursued insects and had not seen any other proof of their existence. Maybe there was something in one of her note-books.

Beatrice slid out of bed and limped over to the dresser. She opened the bottom drawer, where she kept a few of her older notebooks and several scrapbooks. She flipped through them, then stopped when she got to a scrapbook of newspaper stories. They were mostly about Isabelle or Mr. Cecil, but she remembered a recent article that had actually been written by Robert Russel. She found it again and began to read:

The New York Times
Saturday, April 12, 1926

The Russel Hollywood Report

Bigger is always better in this land of dreams. And two of the biggest names in Hollywood are battling to have the biggest theatre. Mr. Cecil's Theatre Eternal and Grauman's Chinese Theatre. It's like watching giants fighting with stone.

On Hollywood Boulevard it took the muscles of 150 men and the power of two steam cranes to lift the black marble pillars of Theatre Eternal into position. The impressive dark pillars were imported from Italy—money is no object in this world of film. The theatre's walls are massive and equally dark and there are no windows. Mr. Cecil planned it that way, for there is no point in having windows in a theatre; it is a place where you gaze into another world. It took fifteen months and over $800,000 to bring the theatre to this juncture, the first crew working all day and the second crew labouring all night under a massive array of electrical lights. When the theatre is finished it will seat 1,333 people, one of the largest movie theatres in the world.

The theatre is being constructed directly across the street from Grauman's Chinese Theatre so that the two are facing off against each other, one orange and white and the other the colour of the darkest dark. Each day they battle for the attention of those who pass by in automobiles, on foot, or on bicycle. People even take bets on which will be finished first. Grauman's Chinese Theatre is the nearest to completion and most who laid down money did bet on that one. After all, this is Grauman's third major theatre. But just last week twenty of the workers and all six of the foremen employed by Grauman fell sick after being bitten by particularly nasty (and—if the stories can be believed—giant) wasps. Two of the men actually died from the bites. The welts were said to be the size of baseballs! The lack of strong backs was enough to stop construction.

Who will win this madcap race? The name of Mr. Cecil's theatre is etched in Latin across a huge slab of black stone that dominates the

front stairs: THEATRUM AETERNUM. But that is
too long and too foreign a name for the public
to use, so it has become known as the Theatre
Eternal. It is a place of dreams.

And this is the city where people dream big.

The Theatre Eternal was completed now and waiting
for *Frankenstein*. It was that line about the insects that had
caught in Beatrice's memory. It wormed its way into her
thoughts. Into her logic. She had discovered giant wasplike
creatures in his cottage. And they obviously hadn't stung
him. And if he could control them, could he also send them
after the workers at Grauman's Theatre?

She looked up at the framed scorpion hornet on the
wall. Last night, Mr. Cecil had seemed to be communicating
with the dead insect. The thing stared at her with its compound eyes.

So little of this was making any logical sense.

She felt a chill, so she pulled on her khakis. When she
opened the stockings drawer she gently removed several of
Raul's drawings and set them on the dresser, then retrieved
the photograph of her father from the bottom. She had discovered the photo in her aunt and uncle's room years earlier,
while she and Isabelle were playing hide-and-seek. She'd
stolen it and a matchbox containing three of her father's
medals from the Boer War—one silver and two bronze—and
squirrelled away her discoveries here.

She lifted up the photograph. It was the only picture of
her father she'd seen. He was holding a calf in his arms, his

sleeves rolled back enough to show his muscles. His face was determined, wrinkled by time and the sun. *Ernest Thorn, 1910,* was written on the back. Only three years before she was born.

She wished she could somehow reach into the photograph to take her father's hand. To be there. In the same time, the same place as him. It was where she truly belonged. But he was forever frozen in that pose, in the past, and she was forever stuck in the present.

She clutched the photo to her chest, then put it back in the drawer. She touched the war medals for good luck. *Superstition*, she thought. Then she snapped up the medal with the image of Queen Victoria on the front and stuffed it in her pocket. She closed the drawer.

With the medal serving as a comforting weight, Beatrice went to the wall and examined the insect Mr. Cecil had given her. He'd called it a *Zebûb*. The name was unfamiliar. It sounded almost Arabian—not Latin, as was used by scientists for naming insects. But Mr. Cecil had said the sting was her first taste of the *inevitable future*. What could that possibly mean?

She was tempted to smash the glass, but then the beast might fly away. It was dead, wasn't it? She took the frame down and went into the closet. Lifting aside Gibbon's *Decline and Fall,* she picked up the tin can. She placed the framed specimen and the can in a pillowcase and set them next to the bedroom door.

A pinch of pinkness had appeared in Isabelle's cheek. Beatrice sat on the bed and took her sister's hand. "I'm going out. I need fresh air. But if you want me just call and I'll come to you, Izzy. You don't even have to call all that loud."

There was no response.

Beatrice carried the pillowcase out of the room. When she was outside, she grabbed a shovel from the garden shed and dug a hole in the soft dirt of the vineyard. She dropped the pillowcase inside and filled the hole, all the while thinking she heard buzzing. She stamped on the earth until it was packed, brushed her hands on her trousers, and went back into the mansion.

She spent the rest of the day and the evening at her sister's side. Isabelle did not wake up.

22

The shades were up and the morning sun brightened the room. Beatrice first felt a throb in the centre of the welt on her leg, then she heard a soft humming and opened her eyes to slits. Isabelle was combing her hair in front of the mirror. Beatrice sat up.

"Good morning, sleepyhead," Isabelle said. Her hair was down past her shoulders, the silver brush made it glisten in the light.

"You're awake!"

"Oh, you're amazingly observant!" Isabelle answered with a laugh. "And I'm ready to take on the whole big, wide world. You, piggietoes, have been snoring for the last hour."

"I don't snore."

"You did this morning, Beets. Thunderous, blunderous snoring."

"Oh. Sorry. How . . . how do you feel?"

"I slept like a log. Like a baby. Like a baby on a log." Another chuckle. "Like Sleeping Beauty."

"You slept for two days, Izzy."

"That's what Mr. Cecil said. I must've been very tired." She stood and did a twirl, her hair flying. "I feel brand-spanking new, Beets. Get up! I ordered eggs and bacon and pancakes for breakfast. Today's a holiday. Maybe we can walk along the beach. Or picnic at the zoo and throw peanuts to the monkeys."

"Did you say you spoke to Mr. Cecil already this morning?"

"Yes, he was here twenty minutes ago."

Beatrice clutched the sheets. "I didn't wake up?"

"No, you didn't, sleepyhead. And we weren't even trying to be quiet. He promised some very special and amazing surprise today. To celebrate the film being finished. Get up, Beets!" Then Isabelle did something she hadn't done since she was a child: she jumped on the bed. And continued to pop up and down, saying, "Get up! Get up! Get up! The morning is zooming by. A day just for fun!" She hopped down to the floor. "It's like Christmas and a birthday all rolled into one."

Beatrice got out of bed.

"What's that bandage on your leg?" Isabelle asked.

"Oh. This? Nothing." There wasn't any blood or pus showing. There was a heartbeat when she almost told Isabelle everything that had happened. But not yet. Her sister had just come out of a coma-like sleep. No sense in troubling her further. "I fell off my bicycle."

"Well, you should be more careful, sis!"

"I will, I promise." She ran her hands over her skull—all those indentations and unsightly clumps reminded her of the surface of the moon. They were meant to be hidden. She carefully tied her scarves in place, letting the ends run down her back like hair. She glanced at the mirror, but nothing had changed in her appearance. She dressed in khakis and a white shirt.

The sisters walked downstairs, Isabelle in the lead. She even slid down the banister for the last few steps.

Uncle Wayne and Aunt Betty were sitting at the main dining table in their matching blue silk pajamas. "Good morning, you lovely flappers," Aunt Betty said.

Uncle Wayne paused between gulps of his orange juice. "It's about time you rascals joined us. The day isn't getting any younger and neither is Betty."

Aunt Betty gave him a playful slap. "I'm younger than you—you cradle-robber."

Uncle Wayne's eyes were red-tinged, but he'd shaved and his cheeks and chin were smooth. "Well, little Miss Isabelle Lazarus Thorn has awakened! Just in time to fill her guts. We're having chicken and pig for breakfast. And fried potatoes. And pancakes! This is not what actors are supposed to eat, but today is a day off. From everything! A day off forever!"

Beatrice and Isabelle sat across from them. Mrs. Madge rolled in a loaded trolley and set the large silver platters on the table: a plate of perfectly fried eggs, yellow wiggling eyes of yolk watching them. The bacon was crisp and the sight of it made the twins salivate at the same time. A mountain of fried potatoes waited in a silver bowl. There were also two tall plates of toast and several jars of Knott's Family Preserves. And a neatly stacked pile of pancakes. It was almost a perfectly normal day, Beatrice thought.

Each time Mrs. Madge swung the kitchen door open Beatrice would glance inside. None of the staff were within sight. It was as if ghosts were making breakfast.

"It's a Sunday dinner on a Thursday morning," Isabelle said. "Sunday dinner on a Thursday."

Uncle Wayne held up a piece of bacon in his already greasy fingers. "Your father would eat this sort of grub every day. Then go off and cut down twenty trees and milk thirty cows."

"Did you have very many meals with him and our mother?" Beatrice asked.

"Oh, when I was a kid Ma would take us over to their ugly little sod house for family get-togethers. Your mom could cook, almost as good as Zhen and her brood. But ol' Ernest was the king of grumps. He once nearly tugged my ear off. He said I'd taken too much sugar. He was a mean, mean old codger."

"Yes, he was," Betty agreed. "He threatened me with an axe."

Beatrice had heard this story a thousand times. The day Aunt Betty and Uncle Wayne had arrived to see the twin sisters and were turned away by The Angry Dumb Farmer with an axe. Beatrice was pretty sure her father had a good reason to be holding that axe.

"Was my mother beautiful?" Isabelle asked. She'd asked this same question ten thousand times.

"Gorgeous," Wayne said. "She could've been a star. Every stubble-jumper in that corner of Alberta wondered how your dad had won her. He must've had some secret sweet-talking side. Or she liked them big and dumb. She was the belle of the prairies." He poked the air with his index finger. "Now that could be a movie title, couldn't it? I should mention that one to Mr. Cecil."

"'The Belle of the Prairies,'" Isabelle repeated. "Oh, I'd like to star in that. As the daughter, of course. It could be a reenactment of my real life. The tragic death of the beautiful mother. The father driven mad by sadness. The burning house."

"And the aunt and uncle who swoop in to save you at the last minute," Betty added.

"Ohhh. It's all coming together." Isabelle clapped her hands. "And the daughter goes on to become a movie star."

"Our life is more than a movie story," Beatrice said.

"I could be the belle!" Betty said, holding her glass aloft.

"You could be the good friend of the belle," Wayne suggested. "The confidante. Or the parson's wife."

Betty slammed down her glass of cranberry juice hard enough that the ice rattled. "Parson's wife? That's stupid. Your movie idea is stupid."

"It's a good one. I'm going to tell Mr. Cecil." He scratched the back of his skull. "I just had another idea. I was going to shoot clay pigeons at the club, but this is even more fun. I'll drive the three of us out to the beach. We could have a picnic."

"That's too much work," Betty said.

He waved his perfectly manicured hand. "Oh, the help will throw it all together. You'll just have to put a bonnet over your hair to keep it from blowing in the wind. I won't drive too fast. I could bring wine and milk for Isabelle. Wine for us, I mean, of course. And cheese and bread and it could be all Parisian."

"Wine would be a nice touch." Betty scrunched her lips together. "Yes, I suppose we can do that. But I need a new cover-up. My old ones have shrinked. Shrunk, however you say that."

"We don't have to swim," Uncle Wayne said. "We'll just be a happy family on a picnic. They'll make postcards of us and sell them to families that don't live our lives. It'll be—"

"A picnic is a lovely idea," Mr. Cecil spoke from behind Beatrice. She shuddered. "But just a romantic husband-and-wife getaway from the children, from all your responsibilities. Perhaps even stay long enough at the beach to watch the sunset."

"That's even better," Uncle Wayne said. "A romantic getaway is exactly what Betty and I need." He pinched her cheek.

Mr. Cecil rested his hands on the back of the chair next to Beatrice. She leaned away from him.

"I'll take the twins for a drive myself, today," Mr. Cecil said.

"Even Beatrice?" Aunt Betty said.

"Yes, especially Beatrice. It's time she started seeing a few things. The real world."

"Oh, that's a great surprise!" Isabelle said. She grabbed Beatrice's hand. "We're going on a trip together."

Beatrice nearly choked on her toast. What would he do to her? To them?

"I had . . . I had an idea, Mr. Cecil," Uncle Wayne said. "A really good one. It's about a film. A prairie idea. I even had a title. It's—it's—"

"Tell me later," Mr. Cecil said. "This is your time off. Forget about films. Forget your responsibilities."

"Oh," Uncle Wayne said. "I will. I will. Films forgotten. Responsibilities forgotten."

"And you two ladies," Mr. Cecil continued. "I want you to be ready for twelve noon exactly."

"How should I dress?" Isabelle was still holding Beatrice's hand. "Will we be taking the open car? Do I need a bonnet?"

"We'll be in the Lincoln. Dress as though you're going out for lunch at a fancy establishment. Please wear sunglasses to hide your faces, both of you. Hats with veils, too. Something stylish but not too eye-catching. We're going incognito."

"Incognito!" Isabelle repeated. "That sounds like we're spies. It'll be a grand adventure."

"Oh, I'm certain it will," Mr. Cecil agreed. He patted Beatrice on the shoulder, then left the room.

23

At twelve noon, Isabelle and Beatrice walked out the front doors of La Casa Grande, wearing sunglasses, cloche hats, and dresses that weren't too flashy. Isabelle had taken great joy in helping her sister pick a grey dress and put it on properly.

Across the driveway, Raul stood halfway up a small ladder that was leaning on a palm tree. He snipped at the leaves with a pair of clippers. He gave Beatrice a subtle wave and mouthed the words: *How are you?*

Fine, Beatrice mouthed back. She managed a half-hearted smile. Fine *is not the right word,* she thought. Dread was in her bones.

"Is he your boy?" Isabelle asked.

"No."

"What's his name again?"

"Raul. You know that."

"Why should I know that?" She rolled her eyes. "He's cute, Beets. I'm so glad you have someone to play with while I'm off working."

"I don't just play while you're gone. And he's not *mine.* At least not in that way."

"The Beatrice doth protest too much," Isabelle said. "Maybe we should take him with us for lunch."

"Mr. Cecil wouldn't stand for that."

"I was joking, Beets. You don't take garden boys to lunch. That only happens in the movies." She chuckled. "Plus this is your big trip out. Who would want to share it with a stranger?"

The Lincoln Town Car came up the paved road from Mr. Cecil's house. Raul climbed down the ladder and disappeared into the foliage.

"Our royal carriage is here, sis," Isabelle said.

Mongo stepped out of the car and opened the door to the passenger compartment. Beatrice peered in. Mr. Cecil was sitting in the back seat, his hands resting on his knees. He smiled and gestured for them to enter. Isabelle, without hesitation, slid next to him. Beatrice's legs had turned to stone. But her sister was in there. She had to go. She forced herself to move, and sat alone on the opposite seat.

The door closed and soon the car was humming quietly along. *I am going outside,* Beatrice thought. *Outside!* The guards opened the iron gates to the estate long before they arrived, so the Lincoln didn't have to slow down. She couldn't decide if the lump in her throat was from fear or excitement. As they turned away from the ocean and rumbled toward the hills, Beatrice sat closer to the window, the buildings reflecting in her eyes. In a relatively short time they were out of Santa Monica and into Los Angeles. There were several little cities packed into this part of California, bumping into one another, yearning to bloom into full-sized cities. The heat of the sun failed to get into the car. The sand-coloured buildings cast the occasional shadow across the vehicle.

"Enjoying the sights?" Isabelle asked. "Just wait, things only get better and bigger."

"I'm sure they do."

The massive white letters *Hollywoodland* stood above them on a hill. "Everything has to be named, doesn't it?" Beatrice said. "That's how you possess things."

"Ah, you are thinking big thoughts today, Beets."

"Don't tease her, Isabelle," Mr. Cecil said. "Beatrice is a creature of logic and observation. And she's partially correct. You name things to make them something that can be owned. But it's a contract that allows you to have the actual possession."

"And is that how you got Uncle Wayne and Aunt Betty?" asked Beatice. "A contract?"

"That's how I got everything," Mr. Cecil answered. "Except you two. For that I owe a debt to the hand of fate."

"We're very lucky," Isabelle said. "I've always felt very lucky. In everything."

"Do you remember the exact moment you fainted?" Mr. Cecil asked. "That wasn't about luck."

The slightest hint of a grimace appeared on Isabelle's face. She shook her head.

"You did some of your finest work right before that. Truly breathtaking. I've not properly thanked you."

"You don't need to thank me, Mr. Cecil. It's my job."

He patted her on the leg. "You did more than your job—

you excelled. You overcame. I'm proud of you. And as a reward I'm taking you both to Café Montmartre."

Isabelle clapped her hands. "I adore the Montmartre! The food is divinely French. Everyone goes there to be seen! Don't you love it, Beatrice?"

"I've never been there," she said.

"I know that. But I'm sure you've heard me talk about it."

"I've arranged a private table," Mr. Cecil said.

Isabelle clapped again. "It's like it's my birthday and Christmas all rolled up into one!"

"You're repeating yourself," Beatrice said.

Izzy stuck out her tongue. "I just so adore dining out."

The car pulled up to Isaac's Haberdashery, one door down from Café Montmartre. There were other fancy cars a block ahead of them and a small crowd had gathered across the street—people hoping to see acting royalty, to glimpse in real life a face they had only seen on the screen. There were several photographers, too.

"Now, neither of you draw any attention to yourselves," Mr. Cecil said.

Beatrice tightened her scarves and made certain her black veil covered her face properly. Mongo opened the car door and Mr. Cecil guided the two girls down an alley and up to a red door. It opened, and a man in a white suit led them up a set of narrow hardwood stairs.

"I wonder who we'll see?" Isabelle whispered. "Everyone comes here. Everyone!"

Another door was opened for them and a waiter in a white vest and white shirt and trousers bowed and silently ushered them to a lone table in a semi-dark room. An ornate chandelier hung from the ceiling, a red curtain covered the wall. There were no other tables.

"This is *very*, *very* private," Beatrice said.

"Where are we?" Isabelle asked. "I thought we'd be part of the scene."

Mr. Cecil smiled. He motioned and the waiter pulled the curtain back. On the other side was a window that showed the interior of the Café Montmartre. Diners were packed into the room, at small tables with white-and-blue tablecloths. All the men were in suits, most of the women wore fashionable hats and dresses. The dance floor had two golden curtains and a turquoise fabric ceiling. Only two couples were dancing. Light tinkling laughter echoed from one of the nearby tables, the sound coming in through tiny holes above the window.

"It's a two-way mirror," Mr. Cecil said. "I had this room built for me."

"You spy on people here?" Beatrice asked.

"No, I observe. Make decisions about who should be in my films."

Beatrice and Isabelle took their places at the table, pink drinks with candied cherries already waiting for them. A plate covered by a silver lid also waited. Mr. Cecil sat with his back to the wall. "I've ordered your favourite meals."

Beatrice removed the silver lid to discover rolled chicken. Isabelle lifted her own lid and gasped. "Strawberry prawns! Oh, this is sinfully delicious and I'm so famished."

"Please don't wait for me," he said. "Dig in."

The two girls began to eat, Isabelle quickly and with a ravenous attitude, and Beatrice much more slowly. Mr. Cecil watched them lunch without saying a word, his eyes seeming as lidless as those of ancient Egyptian statues.

"Tell me," he said after a few minutes, "what's the most powerful weapon mankind has created?"

"Those big bombs," Isabelle answered, shaking a prawn at him. "The cannon things. And airplanes. And warships."

"Yes, they are powerful," he agreed. "And Beatrice, do you have a guess?"

"Scientific knowledge."

He smiled. "You're close. Human imagination is mankind's most powerful weapon. Picture that first painting on a cave wall, seen in the flickering torchlight. The visual memory of humanity. That was the first step toward films. The flicker shows we create now are just an extension. They are dreams writ large. The capacity to dream is stronger than any blockade of ships or regiment of soldiers. Not every sentient creature gets such a rich gift. An architect dreams of a building and the building becomes real."

"Imagination is what allowed Darwin to think up evolution, then set out to prove it," Beatrice said.

"Exactly!" Mr. Cecil said. "Imagination is what feeds the film industry. We use it to create our stories. People leave our theatres with new thoughts, new feelings, and new emotions in their hearts. What if that power could be harnessed?"

"You can't harness imagination," Beatrice said.

He wagged his index finger. "Not true, Beatrice. It's a

problem I'm very close to solving. How to harness fear. But once you've harness it, what can it be used for?"

Beatrice didn't know what to answer. She'd been swept up in his intellectual argument. But as she considered the idea of Mr. Cecil somehow harnessing imagination a chill settled in her stomach.

"I'm sorry, I'm going on too long," he said.

"It all sounds very fascinating and interesting," Isabelle said. "Very much so."

He rubbed his hands together. "Anyway, let's set those imaginary thoughts aside. I brought you here for one other reason. See through that mirror? There are actors at each of the tables, there are waiters hoping to be actors serving them. This whole café is polluted by their desperation. How many late nights do they dream of being on the silver screen, of crowds shouting their names as they walk between the velvet ropes to the opening of their films? So few of them become stars. But not one of them is sitting in this private room, Isabelle."

"No, they aren't," Isabelle agreed. "It's just us!"

"Once in a generation a natural actor comes down from the heavens. Mary Pickford is just such a person. Charlie Chaplin, too. And you, Isabelle Thorn. It isn't just that the people out there in America and beyond our waters know your name. The audience looks at you and sees each character you've played. The Girl Threatened. The Girl Distressed. The Girl in Danger. The men want to protect you. The women want to nurture you. The young boys wish to befriend you. The young girls wish to be you. You've become a symbol to them. Other faces as beautiful as yours soon are forgotten but your face stays in their minds, burning like a sun."

Isabelle nodded as though receiving it all as a sudden revelation. Beatrice frowned. *Why is Mr. Cecil blowing all this hot air?*

"But there's one more reason you're above all of them. I'm guiding your every move. I understand the visual metaphors. What each scene, each image means. How it affects the mind and soul of each human who watches. I can make feeling flower in the coldest heart. Ideas mushroom in the dullest brain."

"Yes, you do," Isabelle agreed. "You can. You are so good at that . . . that flowering." Beatrice watched her sister accept all of this without question. She wanted to argue with him, to somehow wake Isabelle up, but his points were valid. He was the best filmmaker of his generation.

"The change from silent to sound movies will grind most of today's generation of actors into dust. There will be music that plays at the exact moment an actor weeps, not depending on some fumbling half-drunk pianist. But more important, the actors will speak in a film and the people will hear the words. The actresses will sing and the audience will vibrate to each note. Imagine that. Every word you speak will travel to the ears of every man, woman, and child who sits in the theatres of the world. Those performers who have plain voices, who whisper, who rasp will be left to moulder. But you, Isabelle, you have a voice."

"I do?"

"Yes," he said. "And the strongest aspect of your voice

is that primal scream. It's the wailing of the lost child. The fear of the dark. All in that scream. They will speak about *Frankenstein* as the movie that changed everything, and you as the actress who brought that transformation to the world."

"It does sound wonderful," Isabelle said. "The change that changed the world."

Beatrice dropped her fork and it clattered on her plate. "Why did you bring me here?"

Mr. Cecil turned those seemingly friendly eyes to her. "I brought you, Beatrice, because I wanted to do a test run, so to speak. To take you away from the protective walls I've made for you. Just to see how you behave in the open. And . . . I have an announcement." Two envelopes appeared in his hands. Beatrice peered down his sleeves, not certain how that trick had been done. He handed one to each of the sisters.

They opened them at the same time, tearing the paper. Beatrice read the words inside:

Beatrice Thorn,

You are cordially invited to the premiere of Frankenstein *this Friday, September 17, at 8 P.M.*

"I've never been invited to a premiere," Beatrice said. *Is this because he somehow feels sorry for the pain he caused me?* But he was an eloquent man and if he intended to apologize he would use words. She knew that.

"It's time you went to one," Mr. Cecil said. "You'll be one of the stars of the evening."

"It's tomorrow night!" her sister said. "I really have slept."

"I finished the editing much faster than I believed possible. We've moved up the premiere. I don't want anyone else to nab this historically important moment. And I thought it only suitable that both of you be there. You see why I'm inviting your sister, don't you, Isabelle?"

Isabelle nodded. "Oh yes. I get it. It's very symbolic. And fun!" She shared a knowing glance with Mr. Cecil.

What's this all about? Beatrice thought.

"Ah, it will be a night of surprises." Mr. Cecil gestured to the table. "Now enjoy your just 'desserts.'" He winked.

A waiter, as if on cue, approached and set a dish in front of each twin. Beatrice couldn't eat her soufflé but Isabelle finished hers easily. When it was time to leave, Isabelle stood to stare down at all the other patrons.

"I'm above them, Beets," she whispered. "Isn't it wonderful? I don't think I've ever been so happy as I am now."

24

On the day of the premiere Annie, the costume designer, and Megan, the makeup artist, arrived at noon and began their work on the twins. Beatrice had met them both several times because they often came to the mansion with new dresses or new batches of makeup for Isabelle—they were two of Mr. Cecil's most trusted employees.

"Hold still, sweetie," Annie said to Beatrice, a line of pins in the older woman's mouth. "Hold still. I won't poke you too many times."

Then Mrs. Madge brought in two green dresses with galaxies' worth of sequins. Both had long satin sleeves.

"Is one of those for me?" Beatrice asked.

"Of course, silly," Isabelle said.

"But how did you know my size?"

"Sweetie," Annie said. "You and your sister are within a hair of the same size."

"No, we're not."

"A tape measure never lies," Annie answered.

That's not scientifically possible, Beatrice almost said. *We are dissimilar twins.*

"You look like a scared rabbit," Isabelle said.

The green dress fit her as if it were a layer of perfect skin that had grown over her flesh. The sleeves covered the birthmarks scattered across her arms. It was a dress designed to draw eyes toward her. Her hair was still hidden by a tight scarf, her face that same lopsided visage.

"Sit in the chair," Megan said. Her voice was cigarette-smoke hoarse. She expertly layered white napkins around Beatrice's neck.

"I don't need makeup," Beatrice said. "I want to be me."

Megan lifted a brush with white powder on it. "Everyone needs makeup, girl. Some more. Some less. And I can do it all, from madams to monsters. I'm the absolute best. And makeup brings out the real you."

Megan began dusting her with so much white powder Beatrice nearly sneezed. Then other small makeup brushes followed.

"Don't squishy up your face," Isabelle said. "Relax. I've had to do this every day for years. Technicolor greasepaint, face powder, lining colour, moist rouge, under rouge, derma-tograph pencil, dry rouge, masque, and liquid makeup. I've had them all. Munitions, that's what we call it."

"This stuff is explosive?" Beatrice asked.

"Only in the way it makes you look," Megan said.

Isabelle sighed. "It's going to be such a grand adventure today, Beets. I can't wait to see the new theatre. I love theatres! And this'll be the best of them all. I just know it."

"I'm certain it will."

"And the crowds, Beets! It's such a rush when they roar your name. It makes your heart flip. They'll adore you."

"No they won't! They'll just see you, Izzy. They'll be there for you."

"Perhaps." She fluffed her hair. "But you are the surprise. My fans know I have a sister—I'm sure they gossip about you all the time—but none of them've ever seen you. Now, they'll see us together in public for the first time."

That was what Beatrice was beginning to fear the most. The moment of stepping out of the Lincoln. All the photographers and fans waiting, restrained by golden ropes from even touching the red carpet. People would be staring at her! Watching as she rose out of the car, as she walked down the carpet. Her sister had been born to be the focal point of so many stares. But Beatrice had been born to be in the background. Maybe they would give her an opera mask to wear. Then it really wouldn't be her the crowd was staring at.

"Why is Mr. Cecil letting them see me?" Beatrice said. "After all these years of hiding?"

"I've been sworn to secrecy about that," Isabelle said.

"What secret? Don't keep secrets from me!"

Isabelle put a finger to her red, red lips. "Mum's the word. We'll have a smashing good time, I promise."

Beatrice was about to argue the point, but Megan, without asking, whipped off Beatrice's scarves. A moment later something landed on her head and was tugged into place.

"Voila and all that," Megan grunted. She stepped away from the chair and gestured at the mirror.

Beatrice went slack-jawed. The white powder had been used to make her birthmarks disappear. A blond wig rested naturally on her head—looking completely real—the hair falling to near her shoulders.

"You have the same lips as me," Isabelle said.

"And the same face," Beatrice whispered.

"We're twins, silly. It's supposed to be this way. You look just gorgeous. Gorgeous!"

The makeup matched the exact colouring of Isabelle's skin. The two of them stared at the two of them in the mirror.

"I never knew," Beatrice said. "I never knew we looked so much alike."

"You saw the blemishes, girlie," Megan said. "That's all. I took them away."

Isabelle grabbed Beatrice's hand and clutched it tightly.

"This is going to be such a grand evening, Beets. A perfect evening. And there's one more big surprise that Mr. Cecil and me have for you. For everyone. I can't wait until you see it."

25

At six fifteen in the evening, the sun was turning crimson and inching toward the horizon, colouring the grounds of the Cecil Estate red. Uncle Wayne opened the double doors of the mansion and led Aunt Betty and the twins onto the driveway. Beatrice stumbled once and Isabelle reached out to hold her steady on her new T-strap dress shoes.

"These shoes!" Beatrice said. "They aren't meant for human feet."

"Just keep your back straight," Aunt Betty said. She adjusted the strap on her blue satin dress—the dress could have come out of the pages of *Vogue* or *Harper's Bazaar*. "I should've been training you with a book on top of your head since you were a toddler. I never dreamed I'd ever see you this dressed up and going to an opening."

Uncle Wayne whistled. He was in a double-breasted tuxedo with a bow tie, his hair slicked back and his face shaved. "I still don't know which is Beets and which is Izzy. It's amazing!"

"I'm Beets," Isabelle said, raising her hand. "I'm Beets."

All of them laughed except for Beatrice. She glanced around the grounds.

"He's in the trees over there," her sister whispered, pointing secretively. "Oh, this is just like a romance movie."

Beatrice looked where her sister had pointed. Raul was partly hidden by a mulberry bush, watching them. He didn't have a smile or a grimace on his face. Only shock and wonder. The way she had been primped up somehow was making her feel a different kind of power. A confidence. *This must be how actors feel when they become a character.* She winked at Raul.

A long black Lincoln pulled up to the front of the mansion and they all got into the back compartment. The driver was one of the guards from the front gate. Raul was still staring at the darkened windows as they pulled away.

"We're going to a magic place," Uncle Wayne said. "Where the fans scream your name." His eyes glowed with anticipation.

"You look gorgeous," Aunt Betty said to Isabelle. "Gorgeous, child. They'll eat you up. That sleep brought colour to your cheeks. I wish I looked half as yummy as you."

"You are one hundred percent yummy, dear," Uncle Wayne said.

Beatrice felt her stomach turn.

"I forget most of the film already," Isabelle said. "That always happens. I forget the story. It takes place in a castle, I remember that much."

"And I play your father, you haven't forgotten *that*." Uncle Wayne tickled her under her jaw. "Brilliant idea from Mr. Cecil, to have me play a role I already know so well. It makes it all so natural."

"Don't you die?" Isabelle said.

"I die to protect you. It's a very brave sacrifice. Noble."

"I kind of remember that. Whenever I see any of my films it's like it's a brand-new story!"

They rounded the corner of the road and raced full speed out the open gate. Then the car sped past rows of mansions: the homes of oil barons, bondsmen, doctors, lawyers, other movie producers, and the occasional movie star. The traffic grew thicker as they entered Los Angeles: an abundance of automobiles, an abundance of people, the sun setting behind them. They turned right on Wilshire Boulevard. The buildings vanished, and it became a flat area with grass and oil derricks along the road—a park in the middle of the city. Beatrice stared out the window at the La Brea Tar Pits. The pits themselves were bubbling beside the road. "There are monsters in the tar," she said. "The bones of ancient dinosaurs and sabre-toothed tigers."

"A good place for them," Aunt Betty said. "Gives me the chills. Maybe the driver doesn't know the best route."

The car turned north a few blocks later, passing several apartment buildings. Crowds doubled, then tripled. At Hollywood Boulevard they had to slow down for people who were packed together on the sidewalks, spilling out onto the street: men dressed up in suits and tuxedoes and dark hats, women in flashy dresses and dainty little hats. A clown was juggling burning batons. He brought one to his mouth and as the car passed he shot flames into the air.

All those eyeballs turned to watch the car as if they knew who was in there. Beatrice leaned away from the window and scrunched farther into her seat.

They passed a tall building. Down one side was a full-colour banner for the movie. It had the title *Frankenstein* on it and an image of Isabelle covering her mouth with a look of fear. At the bottom were the words: *Now with Cinétone sound!*

"I'm a hundred feet tall," Isabelle said.

"If you're impressed by that, then take a gander over there." Uncle Wayne was pointing out front. "Mr. Cecil has outdone himself!"

Ahead of them was the Theatre Eternal, lit up by spotlights situated along some of the taller buildings next to it. The theatre was made of black stone, and larger than any of the structures around it. It was as if a giant replica of Stonehenge had been fused together and dropped from the air—a place of primeval worship. An electric FRANKENSTEIN sign was stretched across the street from one tall building to another. A burst of fireworks shot through the sky, announcing their arrival.

Isabelle grabbed her sister's hand. "It'll be wonderful. This is what I live for. Now I remember why I do all that hard work." She gave her another squeeze. "You're a star tonight, too. A mysterious, amazing star."

The long car pulled up to the red carpet, the driver opened the door, and Uncle Wayne was the first to step out, taking a moment to enjoy the applause of the crowd. Then he turned and extended his hand to help Aunt Betty. There was more applause, but it seemed muted. Uncle Wayne reached in a third time and took Beatrice's hand. She fought him for a moment, pulling back, then, after a push from Isabelle, she half-stepped, half-stumbled out onto the sidewalk. Her fancy shoes caught in the carpet, but her uncle kept her upright. A spotlight from the top of the theater lit her up and blinded her.

"Oh, *now* they flick on the spotlights," her uncle hissed.

Immediately, Beatrice felt the eyes of the crowd upon her, their cheering filled her ears. There was a flood of *Ooohs*.

"Isabelle! Isabelle Thorn!" a man shouted.

A child squealed, "She's really real!"

The eyes were everywhere. Several cameras flashed, and she raised one hand. She stood as straight as she could, but her legs threatened to buckle.

"How do you feel?" a reporter shouted. It was Robert Russel! She almost went running over to him. But when she blinked she saw that her mind had tricked her. He just had the same colour hair and a similar hat.

"We love you!" a young man shouted. "I love you!"

"Step over to the right," Uncle Wayne whispered, his face locked in a glowing smile. He spoke between his teeth. "Give Isabelle lots of space. Your sister has to come out now. People need to see her clearly."

When Uncle Wayne let her go to reach for Isabelle, Beatrice nearly fell over. She hadn't expected the crowd to be such a physical presence. They were *there. Right there.* Sucking up all the air so that she couldn't breathe. Isabelle rose out of the car and all the eyes shifted away from Beatrice. She felt it physically. They all sucked in their breath at her sister's beauty.

Isabelle seemed to grow taller, the adulation made her back straighter.

"There are two of them!" a woman screeched. "Two of them!"

The flaring of camera flashes became a storm of light. Isabelle waved and many in the pressing mass waved back. Then they all began to applaud. "Let's go, Beets," Isabelle said, latching onto her sister's hand and pulling her along the carpet. People were shouting out about twenty things at once: "Isabelle, stop!" "I want to touch your hair!" "Iwantyoutosignthis!" A hundred pieces of paper were shoved toward them. "Are you twins?" "I love you!" "You'resobeautiful!" The words all ran together. But Isabelle just glided onward, cutting through the words, giving the crowd a perfect smile as their reward.

The twins climbed the stone steps toward the obsidian pillars and the entrance to the Theatre Eternal. Two large doormen swung open the doors and the twins and Aunt Betty and Uncle Wayne swept into the theatre, where the air was cave-cool and humid. The doors closed, muffling the cheering, but there were more people inside staring. One of the ushers led the group through a door marked *Private Balconies,* and soon they were climbing a set of stairs and charging through a set of swinging doors to their private balcony, with eight red velvet chairs and a view of the screen and the audience below them. It was the kind of balcony that royalty would sit in. The audience looked up. Isabelle waved again, but still held her sister's hand. "That was a wonderful entrance," Isabelle said. "It's quite the amazing rush, isn't it? It wasn't so bad for you, was it?"

"No. No," Beatrice said. "I'm breathless, though."

"Ah, of course. I was breathless the first time, too." She tightened her grip. "But it wasn't the same, Beets. The clapping. It just wasn't. It was like hearing the sea in a seashell. It's not the real sea."

"What do you mean?"

"Oh, nothing. I'm just getting jaded." She gestured to Uncle Wayne and Aunt Betty and whispered: "As long as I don't turn into them." Then she lifted her hand again. "Now wave again to our adoring fans. Let them know that we love them and always will."

Isabelle gently waved at the faces below them. Over a thousand of them were down there and every one of them was looking up at the balcony. Many of them waved back.

Uncle Wayne gave a few waves and Betty did the same beside him, giggling with each movement of her arm. "This is the life," Uncle Wayne said. "Any time I feel a little bit older, a little bit more tired, this reminds me of why I do it. All the sacrifices are worth it."

"Yes, they are," Betty said. "So worth it." She ran a finger over her lips.

Beatrice didn't wave.

Hypothesis:
If a crowd has mental energy, then that energy can be sent to an individual.

Proof:
Kings, queens, generals, and presidents have certainly
been empowered by the roar of a crowd. But that
does not mean a real or measurable energy exchange
occurs.

The lights, which were designed to look like torches, dimmed slightly and Beatrice followed the others as they took their seats.

There was no orchestra pit. Not a sign of a musician. The Cinétone would replace all of that.

The door opened behind them. A large obelisk—Mongo—stood there for a moment, then moved aside. Mr. Cecil stepped onto the balcony, his smile catching the light. "Ah, my stars, my stars," he said as he came around to stand beside Isabelle. "You're here to witness your ultimate success." He placed a hand on Isabelle's shoulder. "Enjoy this. Each moment is yours. Your dreams have been fulfilled and every one of those people down there wishes he or she could be in your lives. Your skin."

He looked directly at Beatrice. "And your skin, too, Beatrice. For they all are wondering who you are. Which of you is Isabelle. Minds crazed by curiosity. The stories of *the twin revealed* will be in every newspaper across the world tomorrow morning and that will fill this theatre and others for months."

Beatrice's breath had caught in her throat. Was it possible that Mr. Cecil had planned this revelation of her—of the twin sister—since the first time he'd seen them as children?

"What did you tell the press about me?" Beatrice asked.

"That *Frankenstein* will answer their questions."

"People wanted to see me, too," Isabelle said. "They know me."

"Yes, Isabelle, they're all here to see you." He patted her shoulder. "You're a dream in each of their heads. A symbol of purity and beauty. An ideal. They absolutely wanted to see you." He rubbed his hands together. "Well, there are a few final gears to set in motion. A hundred years of planning will come to fruition tonight. And you are part of it. I want to thank you."

A hundred years? Beatrice thought.

"We'll have a party, right?" Aunt Betty said. "A big party like last time. I so like the parties."

"In a way, yes, there will be a party," Mr. Cecil answered. "And it'll be unfathomably big. Unlike any you have experienced before. But I must go. This will my greatest film. Each moment is perfectly placed. You'll see. And you'll experience what perfection can summon."

He strode toward the door, it opened, almost of its own accord, and he walked through and was gone.

"An un—unfathomably big party," Aunt Betty said. "Oh, that'll be so grand. So very grand."

Uncle Wayne nodded. "Yes, it will."

Beatrice sat back in the plush red seat. The crowd below them continued to whisper, faces looking up at the balcony, glancing back at the screen. But it was not as loud as she thought it should be with so many people. They were talking quietly, in reverence, as they waited for the film.

The torches along the walls of the Theatre Eternal slowly went out.

The large black screen shivered with light and life and everyone fell quiet.

26

The film began with the inkblot symbol of Cecil Productions, and that symbol made the crowd shudder. It was immediately followed by: FRANKENSTEIN, in large white letters on a grey screen that showed a scene of fog. Dramatic symphonic music played from all directions.

Next came:

STARRING:

WAYNE THORN

ISABELLE THORN

A moment's pause, then:

AND INTRODUCING

BEATRICE THORN

"Is that a joke?" Beatrice asked.

"The surprise! The surprise!" Her sister nearly busted out into a giggle. "Just you wait."

The fog cleared, followed by a slow-moving shot that revealed an ancient castle in the distance under a blood-red moon. The viewpoint of the camera travelled high along the ground, over a wooden bridge that led across an impossibly deep crevice. The screen flashed green and the image of the bridge was burned into Beatrice's retinas. The camera continued along at speed, moving faster and faster toward the castle. Then the camera's eye lifted from that low height and soared into the sky, as if on the back of a giant bird. The crowd below them sucked in their breaths as the camera darted toward the one window in the keep that flickered with light, and into the story.

Inside the room was Dr. Frankenstein, a tormented, mad, and brilliant man. It wasn't until she saw a certain shift of his face that Beatrice recognized that Uncle Wayne was playing the part, so adept was his acting.

The intertitle flashed: DOCTOR FRANKENSTEIN'S BEAUTIFUL WIFE, THE LOVE OF HIS LIFE, WAS DEAD.

He pawed at her portrait on the wall. He wept. Uncle Wayne was watching himself on the screen, tears running down his face. The door behind Dr. Frankenstein swung slowly open and a bright light filled the room, so bright that Frankenstein had to cover his eyes. Then Isabelle walked into the chamber. It seemed the very sun was lighting the room she came out of and she walked on the beams of light.

HIS DAUGHTER, ROSELLA, COMES FROM HER STUDIES TO COMFORT HIM. SHE NEEDS A MOTHER. A FATHER. SHE NEEDS LOVE.

Isabelle, the real Isabelle, was staring at herself. As equally entranced as everyone else. "Is it really me?"

Beatrice took her hand. "It is. A part of you. A reflection that is real."

"I've never looked like that before. I have never looked so real. So believably real."

The camera drew tentatively closer, viewing her through a soft focus. Her eyes had never been more expressive. Her face was flawless.

Another door opened behind the two of them and another Isabelle walked into the room, indistinguishable from the first except that she was wearing a dark dress. She stood beside the first Isabelle.

AND HIS SECOND TWIN DAUGHTER, RONA, COMES FROM HER STUDIES TO ALSO OFFER HER COMFORT. SHE, TOO, NEEDS A MOTHER. A FATHER. SHE NEEDS LOVE.

"How is this possible?" Beatrice asked.

"Mirrors," Isabelle answered. "Splices. Mr. Cecil's magic."

They interacted as if they were standing on the same set, in the same castle. It was seamless. Members of the audience looked to the balcony and back at the screen as if they couldn't believe their eyes.

Beatrice joined the story. Became the story. She wanted Dr. Frankenstein to succeed in finding a way to save his wife, to save her sister's mother. Her mother. She wanted the monster to rise, but she knew the doctor was playing with forces that no human should ever toy with— the power to resurrect the dead. What he was doing was wrong, but she cheered for him anyway. For he had his wife's body on ice and if his experiment succeeded, then he could bring her to life and the family would be whole again. He needed his one true love. His daughters needed a mother. The universe had been so unfair to them for taking her away. And his wife, on ice, was Aunt Betty, but she didn't look like Aunt Betty. She gave the impression of a woman who had once been full of love and life. The perfect mother.

This is what my mother must have looked like, Beatrice thought.

To finish his creation, Dr. Frankenstein had murdered a man—a horrible, horrible man who had come to the castle to rob him—a murderer most foul. The poisoned wine hadn't worked, so Dr. Frankenstein had choked the vile criminal. The death was shown in shadow, reflected on a wall by the firelight. But it was the most awful thing to witness. The act of murder was wrong and would taint the monster, dooming the experiment to failure.

The music was rising here, falling there, drawing the watchers deeper into the film, warning them of the coming horror and heartbreak. For now Dr. Frankenstein was truly mad. And he would finish his project at any price.

The screen shimmered and a green light appeared. It was enough to startle Beatrice, to snap her out of the story. It angered her to be aware of herself again, of her quickly beating heart, to again notice that there was a crowd of people below her. All the eyes on the screen, all the minds experiencing the same story at the same time. They were perfectly still, immobile. Statues. So that only their eyes moved, though occasionally a woman would bring a hand to her mouth in fear. A green mist had formed in the theatre, running along the walls and the aisles. Mr. Cecil wasn't beyond those sorts of tricks to create atmosphere. The mist did appear to be coming out of the bottom of the screen, the same fog that permeated every scene of the film.

THE DOCTOR HAS GONE BEYOND THE PALE. HIS HEART ACHES FOREVER. HE LOVES HIS DEAD WIFE FOREVER. AND SO HE PUSHES THE SWITCH.

The switch went up and the lightning came down from the sky, arcing across the highest tower of the castle and sparking along cables and into the form beneath the sheet on the table. The doctor laughed like a maniac. Then something began rising from the slab of stone, but the lighting didn't show exactly what it was.

THE MONSTER RISES. IT IS ALIVE. BREATHING THE SAME AIR AS HUMANITY, IF SUCH A THING BREATHES. IT MOVES. IT SLITHERS. IT SHAKES. IT SLOUCHES TOWARD LIFE AND IS BORN FULL-BODIED.

Here the camera, Mr. Cecil's eye into the story, showed only Rosella and Rona. *It's Isabelle,* Beatrice thought, but she also wondered if this was how they could have been in real life, both so beautiful and perfect.

The daughters now stood weeping in front of the broken body of their father. His creation had struck out against him and thrown him from the top of the tallest tower. The ice was thawing around their mother's body and soon there would be no saving her from her unjust death. Then a formless shadow crossed over the twins and ever so slowly they looked up. The camera showed a view over the shadow's massive shoulder. The monster towered above them and they turned and fled the room.

The camera followed their flight, showing their feet on the steps, one stumbles and the other puts her hand on her sister's shoulder and they run down a long torchlit hallway that wavers and somehow grows longer so that they are running, running forever, their bonnets loosening and falling away, one by one. Their hair flows behind them.

Rosella's face, then Rona's, fills the screen, both faces showing the pain of losing their father, their mother; the tears are real.

ROSELLAANDRONASEETWODOORS. ONELEADSTOTHECOURTYARDANDESCAPE. THEOTHERTOTHEHORRORCHAMBERSINTHE DUNGEONSOFTHECASTLE. ACHOICEMUSTBEMADEINANINSTANT. THEY TAKE THE WRONG DOOR.

Rosella pushes the wrong door, wiping her eyes. She is going down, down a set of spiral stairs and deeper into the castle, into the madness, her sister one step behind. This is the place where her father had done all of his work, the rooms that he had hidden from his daughters. The parts of his mind that he had hidden. Bats swoop at them, latching onto their hair, so that it pulls out even further. Rosella knocks one away, runs even faster. A shoe falls off, is left hanging on a stair. Then another shoe. And another. Until the twins are shoeless, their bare feet pale on the cold stone. The music rises, a mad symphony that mimics her beating heart. Rosella's hair is wild and as she runs down the steps, rats scurry across her feet.

Then Rosella and Rona are in their father's operating room. A place where there are stained tables and hints of grotesque operations, blood splashed along the wall. The camera never settles long enough for Beatrice to tell whether the lumps on the tables are pieces of leather or parts of bodies. It's all there. Right there. Rosella bumps a pail from the table and body parts fall onto the floor. An eye. An ear. A hand.

The monster is close behind the twins, has slouched down the stairs. They have reached the end of the room and it is a dead end. The camera again is looking over the monster's shoulder as it comes closer and closer to Rosella and Rona. And it slows down so that the twins, trapped at last, turn to see their captor, their enemy, their father's killer. There is a moment when, united, hands held, they might be able to overcome this beast. But then all the fears of their young hearts are written on their faces.

And as they turn and look full upon the thing, they let go of each other and raise their hands, their eyes widening as their lips tremble.

Beatrice knows by the light in her sister's eyes that what she looks on is real, or at least she believes it is real. It is worse than a vampire, a Hydra, or Satan. It is unimaginable and powerful. And, in her heart, Beatrice wishes the camera would show her what the monster looks like. She wants to see the horror. To give it shape and size, and to name it.

But no, the music rises. Rosella who is Isabelle begins to open her mouth and to scream. At first it is silent, then the scream becomes real, coming out of the Cinétone, out of the very walls of the theater. And a moment later, Rona, her sister, joins with her own cry so that their scream has become one perfectly pitched scream. It is of absolute horror, of fear. Of all the things gone wrong in the world. It fills Beatrice's mind and Isabelle's and fills all the minds inside the Theatre Eternal and, without knowing it, without understanding why, Beatrice opens her own mouth and begins to scream in reply, to yell her terror, all the terrors of all her life and the theatre is filled with such a sound, a roar, for Isabelle is screaming beside her, and Uncle Wayne and Betty and all the people gathered below them. They become one voice and the very theatre vibrates and the sound they make is sent back to the screen, back into the story, so that, to Beatrice, it seems as though the screen is soaking up their feelings. It becomes lit with green outlines.

Time stops.

Then a second or a decade later the screen changes and becomes a scene of a grey world. Beatrice sees storm clouds and green lightning and a bridge across a chasm. And yet she doesn't stop her scream; she cannot and she is Rosella again, she is Isabelle, she is Rona, she is Beatrice, and the very theatre shakes at the cacophony.

She, Isabelle, Rosella, Rona, and the audience scream forever and ever.

There is a splice in the film of her life, for Beatrice doesn't know when she stops screaming, only that she does and the story somehow jumps ahead. Rosella and Rona are walking, stumbling, hand in hand across a wooden bridge that leads over a deep chasm. Their aunt is standing on the other side of the chasm; their mother's twin. They reach her and it is as if their mother has come to life again and is holding them both. The horrible monster is dead. The sun is beginning to rise along the mountains, catching Rosella's face and she smiles and Rona smiles and their aunt holds

them and as they stand perfectly still a dove takes to the sky
behind them.

Two words appear on the screen:

THE END

27

The crowd was still. No one made a sound. They just watched as the screen became that final scene of a bridge and a rocky world beyond it. But the story and the characters were gone. The place where they all were together had vanished into the ending of the movie.

The torchlights came up. A few people even covered their eyes. Mr. Cecil crossed the stage and stepped up to a large round microphone that had risen out of the floor.

"You are the first," he said. His voice came from all corners of the theatre. "The first to see this. To hear the Cinétone, the latest in film technology. The sounds and the thrills and the terrors of *Frankenstein*. Go forth into the world and tell your friends, your family, people on the street to experience the film. Tell them it is the greatest cinematic creation of all time. You legions are released upon the world. Please bring the news of this story to all of your kind."

A lone person began to clap, then another and another until the audience erupted with clapping and the theatre shook with the thunder of applause.

"That was wonderful," Aunt Betty said. "It was so real. I

was right there in the screen. In the story. It's the way films are supposed to be. And my hair, it was perfect."

The crowd below them stood. They began to whisper to each other. One woman fell over as though she'd been shot. A man helped her up and she waved her hanky in front of her face. Several were leaning on each other. They shuffled out of the theatre.

Beatrice felt as if she'd swum fifty laps. When she had been screaming in unison with everyone else, so much of herself had come out. If she had a soul—and she wasn't certain souls existed, but if they did—a part of hers had been taken and . . . and what? Put inside the movie? Absorbed into the screen? No. More than her soul. Her imagination. Her fear.

Isabelle was still staring at the screen. The crowds below didn't look up at the balcony again, as though they'd forgotten they were in the presence of their stars.

Uncle Wayne stood. "Why's the projector still on?" An occasional spark of light would appear, then wink out and die. Another and another. The final scene of the mountain path remained. Had Mr. Cecil shot several minutes of the same scene and was now running it in a loop?

Beatrice put her hand on Isabelle's shoulder. "Are you all right?"

She grabbed Beatrice and pulled her close. "He frightens me," she hissed quietly.

"What?"

"I remember why I screamed at the movie set. Why I fainted." Her body shook. "I saw Mr. Cecil's real face."

"His real face?" Beatrice said.

"What are you two talking about?" Uncle Wayne asked.

"Nothing," Beatrice said. "Girl talk." She helped Isabelle stand.

"Oh, I'm a girl," Aunt Betty said. "I like girl talk. Tell me."

"It really was nothing," Beatrice said.

"Did you see me on all that ice?" Aunt Betty asked. "It was so cold. But I played the part well, didn't I? And I came out at the end to hold Isabelle and her twin. Just like a real mother."

Beatrice nodded. "I thought your part in the movie was excellent, Aunt Betty. Very natural."

"Why thank you, Beatrice."

"Wasn't that twin thing amazing?" Uncle Wayne said. "I still don't know how Mr. Cecil did it. Half the time I was talking to empty space, but he filled it with Rona—with Isabelle. Every newspaper will go bonkers over that and the Cinétone. We've done it!"

The balcony door opened. Mongo gestured them toward the door. Beatrice glanced back as they left the balcony and saw Mr. Cecil alone on the stage, moving his lips as though he were talking or chewing. He stretched out his hand and touched the shimmering screen.

He reached right into the screen up to the elbow. Beatrice blinked. Had that really happened?

Mr. Cecil pulled his arm back. No, he was just touching it.

Mongo patted her shoulder and she followed the others down to the entrance of the theatre and into a waiting car. The streets were already mostly deserted.

The way she had screamed in unison with the film and the audience still echoed in her mind. It had been unbidden, horrible, and uncontrollable. All of those people screeching as one. She wondered if the viewers had even realized what had happened to them. Or were they too wrapped up in the story? Whatever Mr. Cecil was doing, he would be creating more of those screams. She was certain of it.

What if imagination could be harnessed? Those weren't his exact words, but close. *Harnessed to do what?*

All four of them stared up at the Theatre Eternal through the back window of the car. "I won't ever act as well as I did in that movie," Uncle Wayne said. "Never again."

Then they were turning and travelling down the hills toward the ocean and the mansion. No one spoke the whole time.

28

The moment they returned to La Casa Grande Beatrice went to the washroom and wiped every last bit of makeup from her face. When she was back in her room she peeled herself from her dress and pulled on her cotton pajamas.

Isabelle sat on their bed in her pink nightgown. "When we shot that screaming scene I saw such terrible things," she explained. "Mr. Cecil said I'd see them. He explained that an actor pictures a word as the actor says it, then the word becomes real. The emotions become real. And he told me I would see something worthy of my scream—awful, evil, horrible images. I thought he was exaggerating."

"What did you see when you screamed?"

"I—I can't describe it. I really believed there was a monster behind me. Something horrible. Oh, the words aren't big enough to tell you what I was feeling. And when I turned. Oh, Beets, it was horrible. That's all. So very, very horrible."

"But what was it?" Beatrice asked sharply.

"I can't say, exactly. It was a burning house and I was trapped in the fire. It was a thing with ten heads. It was Uncle and Aunt with only skulls as faces. Then there were these creatures with . . . with stretchy things on their faces. And Mr. Cecil was there in the middle of it all. And his face changed."

"What do you mean?"

"He . . . he looked . . . He looked like . . . those stupid ink splotches."

"Ink splotches?" Beatrice said. "Oh, you mean the Rorschach inkblots."

"Yes. I hate those things! How many times has he stuck them in front of my face. Testing to see what frightened me. But he became one. A living one. Real. Do you believe me, Beets? I know it sounds crazy. But you must. You must believe me."

Beatrice gripped her sister's hand tightly. "I believe that you're telling me the truth. Your truth."

"Oh, good. I thought I was going mad." Isabelle pulled the covers over her legs.

"We're both going mad." Beatrice touched the bandage on her leg through the cotton. Picked at the corners of it. "I—Mr. Cecil hurt me," she said.

"He what?"

"It's a long story."

"We have all night. Maybe forever, for all I know. Mr. Cecil hasn't mentioned shotting another film."

"Well, it started with sneaking into Mr. Cecil's cottage," Beatrice began. She related everything she could remember, describing the inside of the cottage, seeing a hat like Robert Russel's, then feeling Isabelle's pain and dropping the glass jar, releasing the scorpion hornets.

"There was a finger bone in that jar," she said. She had just remembered it. And with that memory came a realization. She shuddered.

"A finger?"

"Yes. I think. I think it was his finger. That maybe he fed it to them." *Or used it to create them somehow . . . No, that was madness. Better not to speak that thought.*

"Why on earth would he do that?"

"I don't know. To bind them to him. Maybe. Or imprinting of some sort. Anyway, it's not important. This is what's important." And she ended, matter-of-factly, by relating what had happened when Mr. Cecil discovered the sting on her leg.

"He—he did that to you? To your wound. And the whole time I stayed sleeping?"

Beatrice nodded.

"But I should have woken up. Protected you. I would have scratched his eyeballs out."

"There was nothing you could've done. Don't beat yourself up about it. What's more important is, who is he? It's like he's been pretending to be someone else all this time. We don't know Mr. Cecil at all. Or what he's capable of. I don't like the theories I keep coming up with."

"It doesn't make any sense," Isabelle said.

"Tomorrow, Izzy, we'll make sense of it all. We need to sleep on it. To see everything more clearly in the light of day."

"You're right. You're right, Beets. I have you, though, don't I? I'll always have you."

"Yes. You'll always have me. I promise. You can't get rid of me."

They clutched each other and lay back. Beatrice glanced at the window, but only the moon was watching over them now.

"In the womb we were together," Beatrice said. "In this world we'll always be together. One way or another."

Isabelle nodded. "I don't know how I'll ever repay you, Beets."

"Repay me?"

"All my life you've been there. When I would come home from the studio, feeling weak, you'd listen to me and make me stronger."

"You're just as strong as me."

"No." There were tears welling in her eyes. "I've leaned on you. I'm always leaning on you."

"I'm your sister. I'm here for you to lean on."

"But that's the thing, Beets. What have I done for you? For anyone? Even my fans. I'm only the face on the screen. I'm not real."

"You're far too real." Beatrice squeezed her hand.

But her sister had a look of determination. "Someday I'll do something," she whispered. "I'll do something that's real."

"Just sleep, Izzy," Beatrice said. "Tonight we should both get a good sleep. To be ready for whatever tomorrow brings."

Beatrice held her tight and Isabelle did, eventually, sleep.

Beatrice lay with her eyes open, staring at the ceiling, watching the shadows cast by the moon. There was a plan behind this movie. Bigger than just making money and getting more fame. Something that was much larger than she could see. Mr. Cecil always had a reason, a purpose for doing things.

She would have a purpose, too. Knowledge was power, she'd read that so many times. It was time to get just a little bit of that power. She closed her eyes. Her resolve brought calmness, slowed her heart and her thoughts.

Sleep came.

29

Beatrice swung herself out of bed at sunrise and dressed in her khaki clothes. She felt her father's war medal in her pocket as she looked out the window. Mr. Cecil's car was gone and she hoped he hadn't come home at all. Perhaps the film was still running, projecting that odd dark landscape.

She was certain that Isabelle, Aunt Betty, and Uncle Wayne would sleep the whole morning or even into the afternoon. The mansion was quiet as she crept down the stairs and outside. Raul wasn't at his cottage, nor was he weeding with his father. She found him in the south garden, sitting on the lion's-head bench with his sketch pad in his hand and a pencil in the other.

"What are you drawing, Raul?" she said.

He stuffed the pad into his front pocket, along with the pencil, and held up a dirt-stained hand. "No one sees an *artiste*'s work until it's done."

"Well, I look forward to the unveiling."

"You are my biggest fan. Along with my father. How was the premiere?"

"It was . . . it was horrible. I mean, it frightened me."

"Aren't his films supposed to be frightening?"

"But this one." A chill ran along her neck. "It was more than that."

"I saw you in your dress. All made up."

She swallowed. "What did you think?"

"You didn't look like you. You looked like a . . . a starlet. But I prefer the old you—this you."

She had the urge to hug him for those words, but stopped herself. "I guess that's why they call it makeup." She rubbed at her cheek as if the stuff would never come off. "I've put together a hypothesis about Mr. Cecil."

"Trying to confuse me with big words?"

"Absolutely," she said. "He really doesn't want me to go into his home."

"We knew that already."

"No, I mean he's hiding something—that's why he was so . . . so cruel to me that night."

He pointed at the sting on his neck. "He was hiding those stupid wasps."

"I mean something bigger than that. He doesn't want us to discover what it is. But something is calling me there."

"What's calling you?"

"A hat."

"A hat?"

"Robert Russel's hat was there."

"Who?"

"He's a reporter. He disappeared the night of the big party."

"So?"

"Well, Mr. Cecil could have convinced him to leave. Bribed him. Or Mongo may have threatened him. Or worse."

"What kind of worse?"

"Well. Murder, I guess."

Raul gave her a frown. "You think he's murdered a reporter."

"Something bad happened. Maybe there's some kind of proof. And I'm certain Jolly was in that room once. The orphan. I think she saw something she wasn't supposed to. And she died from scorpion hornet bites."

Raul crossed his arms. "Why would you think that?"

"I saw welts on her arm."

"You saw her body?"

"I found her just after she died. There were welts that could've been stings."

"That must have been horrible to see." His voice was soft.

"It was."

"I mentioned the orphans to my father once, just wondering why they didn't come here anymore. He said not to ask questions."

"I have to ask questions. I have to know. I need to go back into Mr. Cecil's cottage."

"No," Raul said. "I can't do that."

"I know, I'm asking for too much. But Izzy needs to be protected. He's hurting her. And he's hiding something from me. From us."

"I could disappear."

"Disappear?"

"Yes," he said. "People like me just disappear in this country. No one notices. One of Papá's cousins disappeared from a farm last year after he complained about the owner.

Even here, odd things happen. There are only three Chinese men working in the kitchen. There used to be five."

"Did they get other jobs?"

He shook his head. "I didn't see them leave."

"What are you implying?"

"I have to be extra careful, that's all."

She fiddled with the medal in her pocket. "I just want to peek in his house."

"I won't go in there again."

"But you have to come inside!"

"You didn't ask what happened to me." Again his voice was soft. "You didn't ask."

"What do you mean?"

He held out his right hand. It was lined with red marks and dried cuts. "Mr. Cecil spoke to my father and I got the strap. Papá does it on the hand so I remember as I work all day. That was three days ago."

"And it still looks that bad? I—I'm sorry."

"I can't go in there. I want to. But the next punishment might be for Papá."

She put her hand on his shoulder. "I know I'm asking too much. But I just can't face going back in alone."

"Well, if you're going to beg like that." He said this softly. "I'll take you to the door. No farther."

"I wasn't begging," she said. "And to the door is far enough." She was certain she could convince him to go inside. She led him down one of their secret pathways and back to Mr. Cecil's home. Every flower had been cropped, every blade of grass shorn. They made their way through the cottage's garden.

It was a space with iron benches and black iron lattice-work. Each stone in the dry creek bed was obsidian. The garden had been set in a perfect triangle. Everything was black, including a black dahlia. It was as if they were walking into a world of night that existed in the middle of the day, that denied the existence of sunlight. A fountain sputtered water, but being built of black stone, it only served to enhance the darkness.

The shutters on the main windows were closed. A heavy door led from the garden into the cottage. It was the door through which they'd fled. Beatrice peered in the door's window and saw the shadowed hallway beyond. She gingerly touched the doorknob and turned it, then pulled on the door.

"It's locked," she said. "Maybe we can jimmy a window."

"No. Wait." Raul brushed by her and a moment later the door unlocked with a *click*. "There!"

"How'd you do that?" she asked.

"Magic!" he said, then he waved a gold key under her nose. "The master key. I stole it from my father years ago so I could sneak paper from the storage room. And get soda pop whenever I want." His smile flashed.

He opened the door. Beatrice tensed, but only air hissed out. She took the first step into the cottage.

30

Raul was still standing in the doorway, the sunlight making him bright and almost hard to look at.

"What are you doing?" she whispered.

"I said I'd only take you to the door."

"I can't go by myself."

"You have to," he said. "I'll keep a watch out for you." He released the door and it slowly closed on its own.

She was blinded by the darkness.

Breathe. Breathe.

Fine, then! I'll do it myself. A door was open partway down the hall. Beatrice went up to it and peered around the corner to discover Mr. Cecil's bedroom, which was lit by a small square window. The room was spartan: a cot with a grey blanket being the only bed. She stepped into the room. Paintings of dark splotchy objects hung on the walls, Rorschach shapes that made her feel queasy. Not a hint of colour. Bookshelves lined one wall. The texts were medical or historical or philosophical: Jung, Nietzsche, Clausewitz; all in perfect order.

The cot looked as though it had never been slept on. But all mammals slept, she knew that. He had to sleep.

She touched the spine of an ancient edition of the Bible. She'd never read it. Each time she'd asked to have it in her collection she'd been stonewalled. She opened the Bible. Many of the characters in novels quoted from it. It was heavy and the words were small. So many words. *In the beginning God created the heaven and the earth.* Well, that was a good start. She flicked through a few pages, then set it down. Beside it were *Dictionnaire Infernal* by J. A. S. Collin de Plancy, and S. L. MacGregor Mathers's *The Lesser Key of Solomon.*

She picked up *Dictionnaire Infernal.* It was a thick book, written in French, and stuffed with illustrations of demons and monsters that had human faces and animal bodies and insect or bird wings. She flipped through and came across a page with handwriting on it. At the top was an image of a horrible-looking fly with a skull and crossbones etched in its wings. *Belzebuth ou Belzebub ou Beelzebuth, prince des démons . . .* was what the text at the bottom of the page said. The names sounded familiar to her. Below the image were the notes that had caught her eye. They were in Mr. Cecil's handwriting: *Lord of the flies, Philistine god, Prince of demons. Offspring drawn to this plane. Phalanges needed.* She was curious as to why he'd jotted down those names. And she was somewhat upset that he'd written in a book in ink. She set the book down.

Phalanges needed? It made no sense. *Why would the drawing need finger bones?*

One wall of the room had a closet. She pushed on the

closet door; it slid into the wall on well-oiled tracks. The walk-in closet went back at least fifteen feet, and hanging along both sides was suit after suit, each perfectly pressed. His skin had touched the fabric, his hands had buttoned every button, the same hands that had hurt her so.

She slid the door closed and turned. There was an insect collection along the far wall: giant spiders, praying mantises, moths the size of her hand. That display included all the steps of metamorphosis forever preserved—egg, larva, pupa, adult moth. The collection far surpassed her own; in fact there were several insects she'd never seen before—but none as horrible as the Zebûb.

Zebûb. Zebûb. She ran the name through her head. *Belzebuth.* Could there be a connection? Belzebuth had been the lord of the flies according to the note Mr. Cecil had written. And the Zebûb was a sort of insect.

Next to the insect collection were several larger jars on a shelf, one with what looked to be a black cat floating in some kind of liquid. Another had a human hand, the flesh green, the fingers splayed. There were organs and other body parts in various jars. The last and largest jar was dirty, the liquid a dark green. She looked inside and eyes stared back. A tiny fetus edged toward her and knocked against the glass, its mouth moving.

She took a step back. No, it was dead. It hadn't blinked. It had only moved, pressing its forehead against the glass because something had shifted in the house.

What sort of man keeps a dead fetus in a jar? And where did he get it?

It had to be for scientific reasons. Beatrice took a deep breath, calming her nerves. It was just a room. Disturbing because Mr. Cecil slept here, even more so because he had jars with human remains.

She left the bedroom. It felt as though an hour had passed, but it was likely that only a few minutes had ticked off the clock.

She went farther down the darkened hallway. It was cooler here, and the walls were grey. There were lights hanging from the ceiling, but she didn't want to turn them on.

Beatrice stopped and stared through the window in the door to Mr. Cecil's study. After a few moments of observation, she opened the door and waited. Nothing moved. She took a step inside.

From this position she realized the room was quite wide, but narrow at the end where they had climbed in the window. Another triangle. There were more lights here, though none of them had been left on. A large chair sat in the centre of the room. It hadn't been there on her previous visit. There were straps along the arms and legs. She lifted a strap and dropped it. *It must be a prop.*

She was nearly certain that conclusion was incorrect. But thinking any further about why the chair was there might break her resolve.

She went over to the projector and lifted a scalpel and lowered it. The spliced film was piled neatly along one side of the table. The Cinétone was connected to the projector by cables, so that they looked like two metal insects melded into one. A larger version of this machine had been used to show the film the previous night. But there was nothing further to learn from it. The film was done.

She went back to the sarcophagus. She'd read enough tales about archaeologists who discovered such prizes and how the coffins were often booby-trapped or there was a trick to opening them.

She felt around the back. Nothing. Looked at the front. Nothing. Pulled on the pharaoh's ear. Finally, she poked him in the right eye. It moved inward. There was a *click* and the lid to the sarcophagus opened an inch. She gently pulled it open the rest of the way, standing to one side in case a dart came shooting out.

She peered around the edge. The inside of the sarcophagus was pure gold. There was a showerhead made of gold tubes at the top, a hook a few inches below that, and a grille at the bottom. And it was perfectly clean. It was as if you could take a shower in it.

"Well, Watson," she said, mimicking a British accent. "That *is* extremely odd." The slightest acidic smell burnt her nostrils. She closed the door.

Then she looked at the brown hat. There wasn't a black feather in the headband, even though her memory had painted one there. She sighed. Beatrice stood on her tiptoes to grab the hat. She examined it. Even gave it a sniff. It did look a lot like the one Robert Russel had been wearing.

She found a hair. If it was the same brown as Robert Russel's then that would support her conclusion, but there wasn't enough light to tell the colour. Then she ran her fingers along the inside of the hatband. And discovered a piece of stiff paper.

The card said: *Robert Russel. The New York Times.*

31

Beatrice slowly, reluctantly, put the hat back on the sarcophagus, standing up on her toes.

The presence of the hat doesn't prove anything. That was her brain talking. But her gut said: *Jolly is dead and gone. And Robert Russel is gone. And Mr. Cecil paid money to Sergeant Muckler, who investigated both cases. To cover something up?*

Robert Russel must be dead like Jolly.

She backed away from the sarcophagus, closed the door, her hands slippery with sweat. She heard a humming whirring sound. Beatrice looked over her shoulder for insects, but there was nothing. Then it became clear that something else was making the low noise: a motor was running outside the cottage. She was about to go to the window and peep out when the door to the room swung open. Beatrice ducked behind the desk, then crab-walked out of view. She slowly opened a cupboard door, praying that the hinges wouldn't squeak, and crawled in. No matter how tightly she squeezed, she couldn't close the door all the way.

Footsteps. Mr. Cecil walked directly to the cupboard door. Stopped. If she reached out through the crack she could touch his black leather shoes. Her fingers trembled. Every bone in her body trembled.

"These last hours are more tiring than I expected," Mr. Cecil said.

There was no answer. There were other footsteps, though. She squinted through the crack. Mongo was standing near the door.

"Bring the victual in, please. My hunger demands sustenance."

Mr. Cecil turned his back to Beatrice and walked to the centre of the room. She held herself completely still, so that she became only a pair of eyes. "One week since a full meal and far too much toil between."

One week? A boa constrictor could go for weeks, even months without eating. But it was a reptile.

"Place the victual in the chair," Mr. Cecil commanded.

Mongo walked into the room now, carrying what looked to be a mannequin. Beatrice pushed the cupboard door open a half inch. A band of light fell on her but she now had a clear view of where Mr. Cecil was standing behind the chair. Mongo had one of the men from the kitchen staff in his clutches, as though he were transporting an infant. The servant was not tied up, but was immobile, his arms crossed on his chest. His eyes were wide and frightened. Mongo set him in the chair and had to push him into place. His legs bent at awkward angles.

"This will not hurt," Mr. Cecil said. "Thank you for your services."

She wasn't certain whether he was talking to Mongo or the servant, but the giant man backed out of the room and closed the door.

"Do not fear," Mr. Cecil said. "It's a natural process."

Mr. Cecil reached down and parted the man's hair. He licked his lips and stared for a moment. No, it was more than licking his lips, Beatrice realized. For he was making them extend, his mouth opening impossibly wide several inches above the man's head. Then something lowered out of his mouth. It was grey and long and the only word that came to her mind was *proboscis*. The very thing insects used to feed. It stretched and writhed out of that elongated mouth. It attached itself to the servant's head. He stiffened.

Beatrice stopped herself from screaming by biting her own tongue hard. Mr. Cecil's cheeks sucked in. The proboscis undulated with whatever he was consuming. Mr. Cecil's eyes were closed and his face looked calm. Satisfied.

Beatrice backed herself as far into the cupboard as possible and closed her eyes. She covered her ears to block the sucking sounds.

The feeding lasted so very long. Beatrice risked one more peek and saw that Mr. Cecil had grown in stature, stood straighter and taller. She couldn't help imagining how a wood tick grew as it consumed blood. Then he let out a sigh, and the proboscis went back into his mouth and he closed it. The servant looked to be undamaged, except for a small line of blood leaking down his forehead. And his eyes were unblinking. He was clearly dead. "In the name of the master, I am thankful for this sustenance."

Beatrice tasted blood from where she'd bitten her tongue. She shook, as if she were in an icebox.

She shut her eyes again. Forever. The door to the study opened and closed. Then she heard another, quieter door open, the almost noiseless hinges of the sarcophagus. Gentle hisses were made, like a misting from a hose. *Is that where the bodies go?* Then a long silence. The door to the study closed again. *Gold does not react to most acids,* the scientific side of her mind told her. A fact. A horrible fact. She knew a strong enough acid would melt a body completely.

She huddled inside, shaking violently. She counted to a thousand before she found the will to unfold herself and climb out of the cupboard. She was alone in the room. Even the chair was gone.

There was no sign that anything at all had happened.

32

The waves lapped at Beatrice's tennis shoes, staining the leather, but she kept marching north along the beach.

"What happened?" Raul asked. "I saw Mr. Cecil go in. But there was no time to warn you." He was a step behind. He'd been waiting in the bushes near Mr. Cecil's house and joined her the moment she came out. "Please tell me!"

La Casa Grande stood high on the hill behind them, the white tower casting a long shadow. Her sister slept inside a room that faced in this direction. Despite the sunlight and the heat, Beatrice shivered worse than she had with any fever. She kept blinking. She rubbed her eyes.

"You were right not to come in," she whispered. "Something terrible happened."

The proboscis. The sound of slurping. It was all so perfectly clear.

"What do you mean?" Raul touched her shoulder and she shuddered. Then the warmth of his palm strengthened her. In all their time growing up together, playing in the grass or running along through the bushes, he'd always had a gentle hand. If she had cut her knee on the gravel he had often been the one to wipe off the dirt. And here was that gentleness again. That humaneness. She leaned against him but didn't stop walking.

"It made no sense," she said after several seconds. "It wasn't real. Mr. Cecil isn't . . . well, it was not possible."

"Tell me what you saw."

She met his eyes directly. Those earth-brown eyes would not envision what she had to say. There were no words to explain what she had seen.

"It was . . ." she said at last, ". . . my imagination painting shadows in a cave."

"What?" Raul took his hand away.

"I have to clear my head." She rubbed at the top of her skull. "Let's keep walking . . . maybe to the ends of the earth."

They avoided the occasional tree branch or strand of seaweed and detritus the ocean had coughed up. She thought of diving into that warm blue colour and swimming away. She would grow fins and gills and return to the oceans where all life came from, away from the madness. She would never set foot in the mansion again.

They strode past a large stone fence—the marker for the property line—and crossed into the estate of Charles Huxon, a bonds investor. His mansion had been built to look like a giant Victorian cottage. Even the trees and the horses had been imported from England.

With each step they put distance between Mr. Cecil's estate and themselves. The sand was soft. The gulls swooped over the waves. Beatrice had never walked this far from home before.

"We have to go back," Raul said after a few more minutes.

"I'll never go back," she answered. She had picked up her pace to a jog.

"I have to. You're safe. If I'm seen even walking through any of the other rich men's places and anything is broken or stolen it'll be my fault. It's happened before."

"I'll tell them you're with me."

"No one will recognize you, Beatrice," he said. And she knew this was the truth. "And besides, it won't matter."

She stopped and looked down at her shadow; her scarves were moving in the wind, reminding her of Medusa. "I can't go back. I'm sorry, Raul. I just can't. You go back. You tell my sister to run. Then you run, too. You and your father aren't safe there."

She broke into a run, not waiting for a reply. Her legs had decided that she needed to move. Raul didn't follow.

The presence of Mr. Cecil loomed behind her, over the mansion, over the estate, over all of Hollywood. She had to get away from it. She went along the stone property fence and up to the street, then continued between the rows of palm trees. She wanted to pound her feet until that image was out of her head.

"I'll go back," she whispered. "In a few hours. I just need to stretch my legs a bit. It wasn't real." She thought of Isabelle, alone in her bed. So vulnerable.

If I go back to the mansion, what will happen?

1. I'll die.
2. I'll die.
3. I'll die.

She couldn't call the police and report what she'd seen. Mr. Cecil could pull strings anywhere.

So she kept running, then eventually slowed to a walk. There had to be a safe place to hide. Who did she know outside the mansion?

No one. No one. No one.

No, she knew Robert Russel. But he was gone. And it was logical to conclude that he had met the same end as the servant. His body dissolved by acid and washed down the drain in the sarcophagus.

It wasn't until an hour had passed and her feet and legs were aching that she heard a soft buzzing. Then the sting on her leg began to throb, at times so hard she nearly collapsed. She forced herself forward. The buzzing grew louder. She turned and looked up, but could only make out a shadow that zipped away.

The Lincoln Town Car pulled up beside her, keeping pace. The windows were black. Mongo, of course, was driving, his face sombre. She quickened her pace.

The car stopped, its wheels scraping on the pavement. A few moments later there were footsteps. Someone was now walking silently beside her.

After a short while she turned slightly to see that it was Mongo. The giant rumbled along, his shadow stretched out behind him. He smiled, which made the scars on his face move. He held out a pad of paper and a fountain pen. She stopped. He was so many times larger than her. He could just pick her up and carry her back, but instead he was holding out pen and paper.

The scars were writing on his face. He jotted something down on the paper. He frowned and she thought perhaps he was sad. Or he was concentrating.

"Yes, Mongo," she said.

He continued to scribble. Then showed her what he had written.

Come back.

He scribbled again. *He will consume her.*

She read it several times before the meaning sank in. The wind made her scarves move and again the shadow behind her looked like Medusa. "I can't let that happen."

Beatrice glanced back at the car. The sun on the windshield made it look like it was on fire. "Is Mr. Cecil in there?"

Mongo nodded. Then scribbled away.

You can't escape. So be strong. Be strong.

Beatrice was surprised at the emotion in his eyes. She nodded and tried to picture her sister as she took each step toward the Lincoln Town Car.

When Mongo opened the door to the back compartment, she drew a deep breath and climbed inside.

33

The *buzz* was inside the compartment.

Mr. Cecil was at the opposite side of the seat, his hands resting on his knees. His face was perfectly calm. She may have, at one time, even thought he was looking kindly at her. "Please sit, Beatrice," he said. He gestured at the seat across from him. "You must be tired. Despite what your instinctive responses are telling you, you're safe. There's no danger."

It took all of her will to sit this close to him. To breathe the same air. Mongo gently closed the door, shutting out much of the light.

One of the scorpion hornets rested on Mr. Cecil's shoulder, its tail curling and uncurling. He gestured and it flew into the air. Beatrice jerked up a hand to defend herself, but the insect dived into his pocket. He buttoned it closed.

"Sorry. I didn't mean to frighten you. I know you feel safer without the Zebûb present. I apologize for not putting it away earlier. How was your walk?"

"Fine." Her voice sounded steady. She willed her hands to stop shaking.

"I knew you were in my study this morning. I saw you there. Smelled you. Did you feast your eyes?"

"W-what are you?"

"What am I?" His smile was almost gentle. "Oh, I'm certain your imagination has gone wild with different scenarios. Even though you are so perfectly logical, the primeval side of your brain will react automatically: *danger, shadow, threat.* You might even call me a monster. Or a demon." He paused. "Is that what you're thinking?"

"Those things—those creatures aren't real. But are you . . . are you a demon?"

He knocked on the driver's window and the car began moving. "Surely you don't believe such things as demons exist."

"No. But—but—"

"Rest easy, child. I am outside your hypotheses. Tales of demons are but symbols, stories that mankind has made up to explain that which they cannot fathom. But I'm not listed in any religious texts or book of horrors. I am a simple facilitator. I make things happen. Movies: I make them. Doorways: I open them. I needed the Zebûbs, so I created them."

"You bred them, you mean?"

He rubbed the empty place where his little finger used to be. "No. I created them. They are a part of myself drawn from another place. To bring them into this world, I sacrificed a finger."

"That makes no sense." She suddenly remembered the finger bone at the bottom of the scorpion hornet jar.

"It's just a matter of knowing the rules. They are my will incarnate. They find a way to accomplish the tasks I ask of them."

The Zebûb was pressing up against his pocket as if it wanted out.

"But . . . where are you from?"

"Outside. That's the only way to explain to your kind. Reality is a bubble around you. You feel. See. Touch and taste it. Imagine there are a hundred bubbles pressed together, each with its own reality. And imagine you can travel from one bubble to another if you know the rules. My job is to use those rules. And I'm good at my job. My employer will reward me when His time comes. When enough doorways are open."

"No one employs you," Beatrice said. "You own half of Hollywood."

"I do have an employer. He does exist, despite reports to the contrary." Then that smile again. "Now you know an aspect of me that I've kept hidden from all except a trusted few. You know how I feed. Your hypothesis has been tested. Have you come to a satisfactory conclusion?"

"You were eating his brain."

"You make it sound so uncouth. It's entirely natural. All living things must eat. It's not a particularly painful process."

The car was still moving straight down the road, but the world outside seemed to be revolving around them. "What did you do to Jolly?"

"Jolly was much smarter than I gave her credit for. She realized her fellow orphans were vanishing. She hid and tried to discover my secrets. Instead, she discovered the Zebûbs. They acted instinctively. Sad, for I hate to waste victuals. You know how that story ended."

"So you created the orphanage to feed yourself?"

"I hear the judgment in your tone. Do you know how many slaughterhouses your species has set up on this earth? I created a secure food supply. People with no connections to the outside world. My lower-rung servants fill that need now."

"And Mr. Russel, what happened to him?"

"Mr. Russel contributed in his own way to a greater good. He gave me his strength."

"So he's dead?" Her voice didn't waver. Each bit of knowledge she was acquiring made her feel older.

"Everyone dies, Beatrice. Well, except me. Or my kin. Or my master. But we operate by a different set of rules."

He's dead. He's dead. The voice threatened to take over her thoughts. Beatrice breathed in and out. Once. Twice. Three times.

"And what happened at the theatre. The scream. That horrible, horrible scream."

"It worked," he said. "It's working now as we speak. All that imagination, that fear. Ah, it is too hard to explain. I can only say that a doorway has been opened. A way to pass from one bubble of reality to another." Mr. Cecil slowly rubbed his hands together. "I don't enjoy causing you consternation, Beatrice. It's upsetting to me, in fact." He spread his arms. "You've been revealed a truth about me, but it was your choice. The fruit of knowledge, it is not so sweet, is it? It was my intention to allow you to blithely live through these events. Your part is soon over. You have been such a support—a pillar to your sister. In many ways you are a facilitator, too. She wouldn't have been able to do all the things she's done in her short life without you to lean on every night. Soon you can rest."

"I'm not going to lie down."

"Just rest, Beatrice, when we get back home. Go straight to your sister and support her. She needs your support. She's tired, and now that the film is done she will be bereft of direction. And she has only one more part to play."

She was silent for several seconds. "Don't touch my sister," she said. "Never. Ever."

"We'll leave that for her to decide. Human beings make their own decisions. They have free will. It's what makes working here so interesting."

They drove onto the grounds of the Cecil Estate. The gates closed behind them.

34

Isabelle was awake and sitting up in bed. An empty bowl of porridge sat on the side table. A plate with a half-eaten cucumber sandwich was beside it. "Where were you?"

"A walk," Beatrice said. "I went for a walk."

"A long one. It's almost two in the afternoon. I had breakfast and lunch brought to the room. I'm too tired to get out of bed. Why weren't you here to entertain me?" She said this last sentence with a smile.

"I lost track of time."

"Oh. I see. I had this odd feeling that something bad had happened to you. It was stuck in my head. But I think it's just leftover stuff in my brain from the premiere. Nothing bad happened, right?"

Beatrice drew in a deep, slow breath. "Something bad did happen, Izzy. I found proof that Mr. Cecil killed Robert Russel. And Jolly. And maybe many others. Lots of people."

The words made her sister sit up straight. "What are you talking about? Have you gone crazy?"

"You have to believe me. I went into his study And I—"

"You went in his study again! Why didn't you take me?"

"I—I—" *I didn't think you could handle it.* "It was on an impulse."

"Well, what happened?"

"I saw things that proved my conclusions. Several things. There was a hat. It belonged to Robert Russel. And a sarcophagus with acid." Beatrice sat on the bed. "And a kind of torture chair with straps."

"What the devil are you talking about?"

Beatrice had always used words so carefully. Had loved them all her life. And now they were failing her. "Mr. Cecil eats people."

"Eats people? He's a cannibal?! You're starting to sound a little batty."

"No. No. Forget I said that. I know how it sounds. It's just that . . ." Nothing. No logical explanation came to her mind. Then: "Do you remember the feeling you had—the things you saw—just before you fainted? You said you saw Uncle and Aunt looking like skeletons and that Mr. Cecil showed you his real face and it was like one of those Rorschach inkblots. And it caused you fear, right?"

"Yes." She did look a little paler.

"Those are gut feelings. But they are the truth. More than feelings. They are real. Your gut is trying to tell you the truth about him."

"He's a merciless director. But he's not a murderer, Beets."

"Just trust your guts."

"That doesn't sound like you at all."

"It is. Today."

Miutes passed in silence. Beatrice watched her sister's face, saw her finally come to a conclusion. "Whether he did those things or not, we aren't safe around him anymore, are we?"

"No. We aren't. Do you ever think of going somewhere else?" Beatrice asked.

"Yes," Isabelle said, "to Paris. Or New York. I think about having my own place. You're there, too, of course."

"Away from the mansion? From the set."

"And from Mr. Cecil," Isabelle said. "Just for a while. I need to get him out of my head."

Beatrice laughed glumly. "A fine choice of words."

"Why is that so funny?" Isabelle asked.

"We should leave. Now. Just pack up and go, sneak out and disappear." She went to the window and looked down at the estate. Was there someone moving there?

"Go? Now? Oh, sis, you are being naughty. But it would take me days to pack."

Two of the guards were looking up at the window. She rarely saw them away from the front gates. "You would go with me, wouldn't you? If I really asked. If I demanded."

Isabelle laughed. "Yes, I would, Beatrice. It would be the cat's meow to finally have an adventure together. Even when you're crazy as a kitten now. You must be hungry. Maybe that's all you need to calm your mind." Isabelle offered her the remains of the sandwich. Despite the queasiness in her guts, Beatrice ate it.

They didn't leave the room. Instead they read and played cards and rested. And rested. Mrs. Madge brought them a meal of fried chicken. Isabelle fell asleep early.

Beatrice put the chair up against the door and went to the window, but Mr. Cecil's car was still gone. The guards continued to stand there, the red glow of their cigarettes clearly visible.

Beatrice opened her notebook and wrote down things she could take from the mansion in the morning. Isabelle had hundreds of necklaces they could sell. And diamond earrings. They could pack them all in a bag and maybe head north. Away from the heat. From this place. Maybe Raul could drive them part of the way.

Later, she picked up her collection of newspaper clippings, all so carefully pasted in her scrapbooks. So many of Robert Russel's words were here. But what had his last moments been like? In that same chair? Each of those words taken from his head one by one, sentence by sentence.

She couldn't let that happen to her and Isabelle.

Beatrice shook her head but couldn't get the image of the proboscis from her mind. She lay beside Isabelle, her eyes open. She became convinced that she would have no sleep for the rest of her life. There had to be a way to get her sister out of here.

35

The male voice came through a thick, almost malleable fog. "You are asleep," he said. "As I speak these words you will rise from your bed and take my hand. You will keep your eyes closed."

Beatrice tried to open her eyes, but failed. She hadn't risen as the voice commanded. She couldn't even move her arms. Her left side was now cold. Her sister had just rolled away from her and was sitting up in bed.

"You are a vessel. You are a star. Rise, Isabelle. Rise and take my hand. We are going to see your film once more."

Mr. Cecil's voice was so soft it was almost unrecognizable. "Now walk to the door, Isabelle Thorn, and wait there." *Stop, Isabelle! Stop!*

There were footsteps as the floor creaked on Beatrice's side of the bed. A gust of breath touched her cheek. "I know you're awake, Beatrice. It's best if you just lie there. Do not fight the inevitable. That's what killed your father."

She tried to open her mouth to shout, even to spit, but no part of her body would obey her commands. *Hypnotism!*

"Don't struggle, please. After tonight you'll be separated forever from your sister. That fact saddens me, though sentimentality is a weakness. But contracts must be honoured. Enjoy these last moments. Perhaps relive your favourite memories from your childhood." The blankets were pulled up over her shoulders.

He's tucking me in!

"Now sleep if you can, Beatrice Thorn. Thank you so very much for your years of service."

Footsteps led away from her. "Take my hand, Isabelle. I'll guide you downstairs. We're going on a short journey. You have one more role to perform. Your most important role."

The main doors opened. Then came the *thunk* of a car door and the sound of the Lincoln Town Car's engine revving. The car pulled away.

Beatrice lay for what felt like hours, feeling her sister get farther and farther away. She couldn't even lift her little finger. Maybe it was better for her to just lie there. She couldn't fight such a powerful man. No, he was more than a man. He was something she could not name. Could not classify.

A facilitator.

He had somehow bound her will. But she had control of it. Of her imagination. Of her spirit. And she would rise above it. Fight it. She visualized herself breaking bonds, iron chains they had put on gods, like Hercules. It was as simple as sitting up.

It took all her strength, all of her will to concentrate. To conceptualize. That was it. Make the concept of waking up a reality. And she did open her eyes. The room was dark, except for the moonlight casting shadows on the wall. She slowly pushed her blankets back and forced herself out of bed.

She dressed awkwardly, imagining she was cladding herself in armour. The chair that had blocked the door was broken.

Beatrice crept down the stairs. The main hall was awash with shadows. Her heart thudded. She went into the west wing of La Casa Grande. The door to her aunt and uncle's room was open and she peeked in.

A childlike whimpering came from inside the room. She froze. A quiet sob was followed by a deep moan. Beatrice crept into the room. Her aunt was asleep in the bed, a sleep mask over her eyes.

The door to the ensuite bathroom was open a crack and dim yellow light leaked out. A stranger was seated on the marble floor in his bathrobe, his hair wet as though he'd been out in the rain. His eyes were dark with black bags below them. It took a moment for her to recognize Uncle Wayne. He wiped away his tears with a golden towel then let out another low moan. "Oh, Lord," he said. "Oh, no. Oh, Lord, no."

Beatrice pushed the door open. "Uncle Wayne." Her voice was hoarse. "Uncle Wayne."

He looked up. His face was so swollen it seemed as though he'd been beaten. "Oh, it's you. You're not dressed up anymore. You're ugly again, Beets."

"Beets is Isabelle's nickname for me."

"Oh, I'm sorry, Beatrice." He did sound genuine. He blew his nose in the towel. "I'm not myself right now, I'm not me. Something terrible has happened. It's all over."

"What's all over?"

"Everything. I'd convinced myself that the party would never end. But he's shutting it all down. He told me that tonight."

She leaned against the door jamb. "What do you mean?"

"The bright lights. The people wanting your autograph. The adoration. Oh, the adoration. I always felt so big. Larger than life. Fifteen years, I've had of it. Fifteen years is what he promised me. And, well, fifteen years have passed."

"Mr. Cecil promised you fifteen years of fame?"

"Yes. And he made it happen. He pulled the strings and it became real. But soon it'll all be gone."

"But what's gone?"

"Mr. Cecil said that our contract was finished. Done. He thanked me for my service." He sniffled. "I'm all used up. And I'll never act as well as I did in *Frankenstein*. It was perfect—I was perfect. Everything in that movie was perfect."

"There'll be other films, Uncle Wayne. You don't have to rely on him."

"No. This was the last one. You're a kid. You don't understand. Mr. Cecil has made the perfect film. He's been sharpening his craft for years and now he's done it."

"But other directors will make films," Beatrice said. "You're a famous star. You can work with them."

His laugh turned into a phlegmy cough. "No one but Mr. Cecil can get me to act that way." He lifted a palsied hand, then stared at his palms. "Are these real?" He buried his face in the towel. "I traded away everything. Ha-ha. I'm a Faust. Aren't I? Faust, the damned." He peeked out at her. "Do you know who that was?"

"I've read the play."

"You word worm. Well, I traded myself. I even traded you, I guess." He let out a wet sigh. "I've been a terrible father. I didn't protect either you or Izzy. I let it all happen because . . . because of the adoration. It's so wonderful when people love you. You'll never know that, Beets. Sorry. It's a hard truth."

"I don't need to know."

"I suppose you don't." His next words were muffled. "I started all this. I showed him the picture of Isabelle as a baby. My sister cut it out of the *Lethbridge Herald* and sent it in a birthday card. When I saw Izzy's picture I knew, I just knew Mr. Cecil would love her face. That it was the face he was looking for. Oh, if only I'd burned that clipping. He—Mr. Cecil killed your father."

"*What?*"

"At least I think he did. Things happen for Mr. Cecil. He makes them all happen somehow."

Beatrice tightened her hands into fists. "How did he kill Father?"

"We went there, Beets. I'm sorry. Beatrice. Beatrice. Beatrice." He took a raspy, deep, wet breath. "When the three of us went to visit you babies we offered to care for both of you. We promised your father the moon and the stars and the old bull got all angry and waved his axe at the car and dared to shout at Mr. Cecil.

"We holed up in a hotel in Lethbridge and waited. I didn't ask Mr. Cecil what we were waiting for. The next day there was that fire and the two of you were found outside the house. Your father'd had his stubborn back broken by a falling timber. It looked like an accident. But it wasn't. You see, there are no accidents when Mr. Cecil is involved. It became part of his plot line. Yes that's it. He controls the plot line."

She stood straight. "You mean he started the fire?"

"He didn't leave his room. But he manifests things. That's the word he uses. Manifesting destiny, he says. Manifesting reality. I've learned not to ask questions about the things he does."

A different life on the farm had been taken away from her, by this weak man and by Mr. Cecil. Her father had been taken away from her. And her sister.

"Can you forgive me?" Uncle Wayne asked. He wiped his nose on his bathrobe. "I tried, I really tried to be a good father. Can you forgive me?"

His body had shrunk in the last few hours. He had always been small, she realized.

"No," she said simply. "I don't forgive you. Mr. Cecil has taken Isabelle. I don't know what he's going to do to her. You could come with me and we could save her."

Uncle Wayne grinned a horrible grin. "There's no point. He always gets what he wants."

"He won't this time." She said this with as much certainty as she could muster. "Tell me what he's doing."

Uncle Wayne shrugged. "I don't know. I didn't want to know. It's better that way."

"Get up. You can fix this. Come with me and we can stop him."

"There's no point."

"Then you're no use to me."

"Your father thought I was useless, too." He wiped his nose again with the back of his hand. "Maybe Mr. Cecil didn't kill your father, after all. I mean you're his blood, right? So in some ways old Ernest is still alive. But you'll disappear, too."

She turned away from Uncle Wayne. She no longer even wanted to be in the same room. He was not her family. Her aunt had slept through the whole conversation, or pretended to.

She walked down the hall and went outside, past the pool, and through the Pomona garden.

We are going to see your film once more, Mr. Cecil had said. She was certain he'd taken Isabelle to the theater.

You'll disappear, too. Her uncle's words followed her like flitting insects.

36

The light of the moon outlined the orange groves. Beatrice dashed through them, the wind whispering along the leaves. She passed the lion bench and ran through the zoo. The monkeys called to her and the flamingo let out one sharp *squawk*. But she didn't stop until she was standing at Raul's cottage. She'd been inside once, a year earlier, when Raul had shown her several of his drawings. She knew which room was his.

He had left his window open, the coolness of the night slipping into the house. She crept up and peeked over the sill. His drawings, in colour and charcoal, were neatly displayed on the wall. There were oranges, statues, the ocean, and even a sketch of her and Isabelle standing next to the lion's cage at the zoo. She wished there was time to look at them properly.

Raul was sound asleep.

"Psst," she whispered. "Psst."

Raul didn't stir. It seemed inappropriate, unladylike to crawl in his window, not that she called herself a lady. So she picked up a rake leaning against the wall and prodded him with the handle.

After she had poked him gently twice to no effect, she gave him a hard jab in the ribs. He stirred enough to bat the rake away. She jabbed it even harder into his stomach and he sat right up, holding his side. He blinked several times, wiped his eyes, then saw her in the window. "Beatrice," he said. "What the heck are you doing?"

She shushed him. "Get dressed. Get out here. With me. I'll tell you what I saw in the study."

A minute later he climbed out the window and she took him by the hand and led him to the orange grove. "What is it?" he asked. "Have you been hurt?"

"I'll try to explain." She found herself starting with *Frankenstein*. "After the premiere was done, Mr. Cecil, he put his hand right into the screen."

"What? Through it, you mean?"

"Into it. As though, I don't know, as if it were a doorway. A place he could enter. Or a place where something else could walk through."

"But I don't understand."

"And in the study. It's where he kills people." She decided to leave out the part about the proboscis. "I found proof. I saw it."

"Saw it."

"Yes, he killed that young Chinese servant. And he uses that sarcophagus to get rid of bodies. That's why they've disappeared. And maybe that's his plan for Isabelle."

Raul paused before speaking. She knew he was putting his thoughts in order. He was probably still waking up, too. "What can we do?"

"He's taken Isabelle back to the theatre. He said she had one more role to perform."

Raul grabbed her hand and pulled her to the garden shed. Waiting beside it was the black Model T truck, with wooden slats around the truck bed. Several crates of oranges were stacked in the back.

Beatrice climbed in the passenger side, watched as Raul pulled on the choke, adjusted two levers by the steering wheel, then turned the key. The truck fired into life. The sound was loud enough to shake the trees.

"It smells like oranges in here." Beatrice rolled down the passenger window.

"It's the orange truck," he said.

The truck jerked ahead, shot up an embankment and onto the road. Raul cranked the wheel just before they drove into the ditch. Then they raced along the estate's back lane until it met the main road.

The security gates were lit by several electric lights and even from a distance it was clear that they were closed. At the sound of the approaching truck the guards came out.

"Just smash through!" Beatrice shouted. "Go! Go! Give it gas!"

Raul jammed the pedal to the floor and the truck sped up. The guards leapt out of the way as the truck crashed through, snapping the gates open. One gate flew several feet in the air and tumbled into the ditch.

"It was like a film!" Beatrice said. "But real. But real. My heart is—"

"Beating fast," Raul said. "I know. I know."

Then a moment later she yelled, "Turn! Turn!"

They had reached the pier, passing the Looff Hippo-drome. Raul cranked the wheel and the tires squealed as the truck sped onto Santa Monica Boulevard. They began climbing away from the ocean and up toward the hills. Raul turned the wheel sharply again and Beatrice found herself thrown against him as again they skirted the edge of the road before Raul got them back into the middle of the lane. "I've never gone this fast before," he said. Beatrice looked behind. No one was following.

"I think we just go straight for a while," she said.

"Shouldn't we tell the police?" Raul asked.

"We can't trust them. Mr. Cecil pays them off."

He took a moment to consider this. "Then which street do we take?"

"I'll know it when I see it."

They went through Beverly Hills, the road getting longer and longer. Had it taken this long to drive to the the-atre? Already that seemed like days or even weeks earlier. There were more stores and shops the farther they went, power lines atop power poles on both sides of the street. The city was asleep.

Then she saw the sign for La Brea Avenue and shouted, "Turn here! Turn left! To the left!"

Raul cranked the wheel again. It was so late at night that there was very little traffic. Beatrice looked at the houses they passed. The windows were black. The build-ings, too. It would be easy to convince herself that this was a deserted city. The occasional car passed. If the police did stop them, how would they explain what they were doing?

They turned onto Hollywood Boulevard and Raul raced the truck to the front of the Theatre Eternal and slammed on the brakes. The vehicle jumped the curb and Beatrice was bumped high enough to nearly hit the roof. She landed, the air knocked out of her lungs. Raul pushed open his door and grabbed Beatrice by the arm, helping her down. The two of them stood there looking up at the theatre. The building was a black monolith in the night, leaning over them, swallowing the stars and the sky. A dim light shone from the glass of the front doors. They ran up the steps, Beatrice in the lead. She yanked on the handles but the doors were locked. She set her feet to put her weight into it.

The smashing of glass startled her. She turned to see Raul had knocked out a panel with a small hammer. He reached inside and opened the door.

"Good job!" Beatrice said. "Let's hope no one heard that." She charged in and Raul followed. It was humid. The dim light was coming from a door that led into the auditorium.

"What do we do about Mongo?" Raul asked. "And Mr. Cecil?" He was still clutching the hammer.

"I don't know," Beatrice answered. "Let's go that way." They went up to the door and crept in. The seats were empty. A ghastly light glowed from the screen. It showed the same mountainous scene from the end of the movie, a precarious wooden bridge that led across a chasm. Across that bridge there was now a dead landscape. What had looked like trees had twisted into snakelike shapes trying to find light, leaves as black as bats flapping in the wind. Pits filled with tar bubbled here and there.

They walked slowly down the aisle, looking left and right. With each step a stronger smell of sulphur filled their nostrils.

About halfway down the aisle, Beatrice held up a hand and pointed. Mongo was slumped in a seat, motionless. Beatrice crept over to him.

"What are you doing?" Raul whispered.

She didn't answer. Mongo's eyes were open, reflecting the dim light of the screen. He did not look peaceful. There was a wet spot on the top of his skull that leaked the slightest bit of grey slime. His mouth was open. There was only darkness where his tongue should have been.

"He's dead," Beatrice said. "Mr. Cecil took everything from him."

The hammer shook in Raul's grip.

Beatrice backed away and glanced around the theatre. It seemed empty. They climbed onto the stage. It grew colder with each step and the sulphur smell thickened. The two of them stopped a foot away from the screen. There was a narrow ledge of rock in front of them and the chasm looked so close they could almost fall into it. Right there on the other side of the screen.

As Beatrice stared more closely she saw there was something winging through the air in the distance. And the path that appeared right at her feet on the screen crossed the bridge and weaved through the landscape and turned a corner out of sight, leading to another place.

"We aren't casting any shadows on the screen," Raul said. He had turned to look back toward the projector room.

"You're right."

Beatrice moved her hand. She and Isabelle used to make shadow puppets on blank movie screens. Now it was as if the light was also coming from inside the screen.

She pressed her hand against the fabric. She felt as if she were pushing on something gauzy and soft, then her hand grew much colder. Her fingers tingled and went through. The air was colder on the other side. "This is where all the cold is coming from," she said.

Raul tentatively lifted his hand to the screen and pushed it through. "This isn't real. This can't be real."

"It is. Somehow it is."

Mr. Cecil had once said there were many realities pressing against one another like bubbles.

She pulled her hand back. The clouds in that other place were moving over a blood-red moon. But her hand had been in another world, she could tell by the tingling in her fingers. She stepped away from the screen and spotted her sister's shawl lying on the stage. Beside it were Mr. Cecil's gloves.

"I think they're in there," Beatrice said. "I'm certain of it. Where *there* is, I don't know."

She turned to look back at the theatre, the empty seats, her eyes blinded momentarily by the light from the projector. "We destroy the projector. We break it and maybe that will stop all this from happening. That must be the way."

"I'd argue against doing that." The voice came from behind them. Beatrice turned to see Mr. Cecil at the entrance to the auditorium. "You would trap your sister forever on the other side of the screen."

37

"Your sister has gone to that other place. Into purgatory. Perdition. Limbo." The door to the theatre closed behind Mr. Cecil. He walked past Mongo without a glance toward him. "She's bringing back someone who is very important to me."

Beatrice waited until he had climbed to the stage and was a few feet away, then launched herself at him, her arms out, her fingers curved into claws aiming for his eyes.

But Mr. Cecil, without seeming to move, was now a few feet to the side. She hit the floor hard. "I've not survived all these years by accident, dear Beatrice. Not without developing certain skills." She pushed herself up. Raul was already standing protectively beside her, one hand raising the hammer as if he were about to attack. "Please don't harm yourselves further."

Then Mr. Cecil said a single word. It was not a word Beatrice recognized, but it snapped her to attention and she rose to her feet, without controlling her own actions. Raul dropped the hammer and was frozen in his pose beside her, blinking and clearly frightened.

"Did you know there are words that speak directly to your cortex?"

Mr. Cecil said another word, a different word that was both familiar and unfamiliar to Beatrice. She found herself moving, her limbs jerking her down to the front row and into a seat. Raul awkwardly fell into a seat beside her.

"Words can be so very powerful," Mr. Cecil said. "'In the beginning was the word.' And from that, all else sprang forth."

He stopped in front of her and looked down. "You've pursued me, Beatrice. You and the gardener's son have mounted your offence. A very curious and improbable effort. And very brave, too. And yet it is of little matter and causes me neither joy nor aggravation. I am uncertain what you hoped to accomplish by coming here—perhaps to stop some imagined nefarious plan."

"*I wahnt mah sssishter back,*" she hissed, the words tumbling out. Her mouth was at least partially working.

"Ah, you grow frightened when she isn't leaning on you. Well, your sister is about to be revealed. In fact, I'll join you for the show." He sat down beside her. "It's fitting that you're here. For this story does deserve an audience." He gestured at the screen. "I do find it curious that you exist though, Beatrice, for you were never meant to live."

What do you mean? she wanted to ask, but her lips wouldn't move.

"When your father was marked to die in a tragic but explainable accident, I'd given instructions to the Zebûb that only Isabelle should live. You would always be the twin who had burned to death. The tragic twist. But your father

226

flouted me. You flouted me. And I decided to let you live."

You were there? She thought, *Are you reading my mind?*

"I am not reading your mind," he said. "So much as measuring the specificity of your thoughts. But yes, I was there. I observed it all through insect eyes. Perhaps I felt a moment of pity. No—I saw a different use for you. The pillar." He glanced up at the screen. "But here . . . here she is. Isabelle returns. And she is bringing along a familiar friend." He paused. "Or a friend familiar."

Two figures inside the screen were coming toward them along the mountain path. The first was Isabelle. She was in her pink nightgown, her hair unbound, the winds of that other place shifting it back and forth. As they drew closer it became clear she was talking animatedly to the person she was walking beside.

That man had brown hair sprinkled with grey, his suit jacket was brown. He carried himself with ease.

"It's you," she whispered. "Somehow it's you."

"It's one of me," Mr. Cecil said. "We are drawn toward the warmth and life of this world. The ideas. We will build a thousand Theatre Eternals. Every human eye will watch this film. Then we will open more doorways. My projectors will bring others of my kind across the chasm between our worlds. Our realities. And finally, when the way has been properly prepared, Master will come."

"You are here and you are there," Raul said. His voice wasn't slurred.

"Yes, Raul, never has a simple observation said so much," Mr. Cecil said. "I am here and I am there. Now I am in two places at once. Soon I will be in four. Then eight. Then I will be legion."

Isabelle was walking closer and closer. She strode across the frail wooden bridge that traversed the chasm without even casting an eye into those depths. She was still talking non-stop, but Beatrice could not hear a word of what she was saying. The man was Mr. Cecil's exact image, down to the nose and perfectly calm eyes. *"Ishabelle!"* Beatrice attempted to shout, but the words were garbled and hoarse. *"Ishabelle. Run. Get out of there!"*

Mr. Cecil patted Beatrice's shoulder. "Spare yourself the effort. She isn't here. She is there. We're watching it all on a film. Watch. Watch."

The two characters stopped at the edge of the screen. Isabelle looked directly at Beatrice, but didn't seem to be able to see through the screen.

"The space she exists in at this moment is imagination," Mr. Cecil explained. "Imagination is the membrane between the multitude of realities. It's both real and not real. A place of potential. All borders are like that. But borders can be very difficult to cross. Isabelle can cross because she has crossed so many times in her films. It's natural for her." He let out a breath. "I wish I could avert your eyes for you. This is where he devours her. You see, in order for my twin to cross into your realm something perfect must die on the other side. All those years ago when I crossed over, just one butterfly was enough. Today, Isabelle is the butterfly. Her death will open the doorway. That will give my doppelgänger the strength to stand on this side."

Mr. Cecil's twin turned. Isabelle stopped talking. The other Mr. Cecil grabbed Isabelle by the shoulders. His face was elongating, his proboscis slithering out of his mouth. Isabelle began to go pale. *It's just like one of his movies,* Beatrice thought. And now Isabelle was turning around and clearly screaming.

"*Shtop it!*" Beatrice shouted. "*Shtop hurthing her!*"

The other Mr. Cecil was attempting to feed on her head, but Isabelle pushed at him. She was not strong enough to break his hold. The other Mr. Cecil's mouth moved and a moment later sounds came out in some guttural language.

Mr. Cecil stood and walked up the steps on the side of the stage to stand near the screen. He was communicating with his brother, his twin. He didn't say anything aloud.

Then Beatrice remembered her own way of communicating with her sister. Her twin sister.

She opened her mind to Isabelle.

There was nothing. The screen was a wall between them. Nothing.

Isabelle lost her hold on the other Mr. Cecil and he twisted her around and attached his proboscis to her head.

No! Beatrice sent herself toward the screen, not her body but her thoughts. That connection between her and Isabelle flicked on like a switch and sudden dread came over her. A sense of powerlessness. Of surrender. She was feeling her sisters' feelings. She was there with her and yet in the chair.

You are stronger than this, she said.

"*Beatrice? Beatrice! Is that you?*" Isabelle whispered.

Yes. Don't speak. Let him think you're growing weak. Then I want you to strike at him, to fight.

Fight?

Yes. Like a tigress. Like Cleopatra.

Isabelle relaxed and the other Mr. Cecil pushed himself closer.

It was as if the proboscis was digging into Beatrice's skull. Into her brain. A sharp pain.

Now.

Isabelle reached up and grabbed the proboscis, ripping it from her skull. Then she smashed his cheek with her elbow. Mr. Cecil's twin was knocked back a few steps and his mouth opened in a silent roar, his proboscis whipping around. Beatrice heard the terrible sound through her sister's ears. It was the scream of a maddened beast. Of approaching death.

Now run for the way out, Beatrice thought.

Which way? Which way?!

Mr. Cecil turned and glared at Beatrice. "What are you doing? Stop your meddling."

"Raul," Beatrice whispered.

"Yes."

"Can you move?"

"A little."

"Go and smash the projector. Smash it to tiny pieces."

"Tiny little pieces," he said. "I promise."

Turn to your right. Beatrice sent the thought to her sister.

Isabelle turned. *Now run, sister. Run straight in that direction.*

And Isabelle threw herself into the screen, but the world held her there, the screen stretching out. For a moment it looked as if she would be pulled right back, but she burst through and collapsed on the stage. The other Mr. Cecil was at the screen, pushing against it. His hands came through but he clearly couldn't go any farther. He banged against the barrier between worlds. There were bloodstains on his face, his proboscis retreating into his mouth.

"Get back in there!" Mr. Cecil shouted. He lifted Isabelle and pushed her toward the screen. "I command it!"

Beatrice found that, bit by bit, she could stand. She leaned on the seat for a moment, wooziness fogging her brain. She picked up the hammer from the floor where Raul had dropped it.

Play dead, Izzy, she thought. *Pretend you weigh a thousand pounds.* She didn't know if her sister could hear her. But Raul was standing now, too, and stumbling up the aisle. "Go," she whispered. "Find something heavy and break that machine."

Then she slouched toward Mr. Cecil, who was bent over her sister.

"Keep your hands off her," she shouted, surprised at how forceful and clear her voice was. She raised the hammer. Hadn't her father shaken an axe at him? But as she pulled back her arm to swing, Mr. Cecil turned and caught her by the wrist.

"Enough of your interruptions," he said.

At that same moment his twin was reaching through the screen and he grabbed Beatrice, too. Both were pulling on her. Mr. Cecil let go and she stumbled back but clutched his lapel and pulled him along in the direction of the screen.

He struggled to stay out of the other world.

BANG.

The world shook. It was a noise that made the screen wobble, and Beatrice turned enough to see that a crack was spreading across the sky of that other world. Then another *BANG* and a *BANG*. It was as if a god were blotting out the sky. Hammer blow by hammer blow he was knocking out the sky.

Raul was destroying the projector. Each blow broke another part of the world. She tightened her grip on Mr. Cecil. Her face was being pulled into the screen. His twin, confused and hungry, began to pull both of them in.

Mr. Cecil grabbed Isabelle. "She'll come with me. The process will not be stopped."

The chasm behind them on—in—the screen was real. Beatrice was certain of that. And if it was real, then the twin Cecils could be pushed down there. She would have to throw herself at them.

Then Beatrice knew something in her heart: she was the only one who could do this, make this sacrifice. Raul obviously cared for her, but he would one day find another and he had his father to care for, oceans to cross. And Isabelle, as strong as she had been this evening, was not a girl of action. Things were done for her, or she followed lines in a script. And millions of people would miss her. *No, it is me who has to go,* Beatrice thought. *To take them down into the chasm.* All these thoughts rushed through her head like comets.

She planted her feet. Grabbed hold of both her enemies. Prepared to throw herself into the abyss.

I'm stronger than you think.

The voice was in Beatrice's head. She believed it was her own thought, but then she felt Isabelle's hand pulling hers. "Stay here!" Beatrice said. "I have to do it!"

"No, Beatrice!" Isabelle said. "I want to finally do something real. It's my turn."

Isabelle pushed Beatrice so hard that she slipped out of the clutches of Mr. Cecil and his twin as both were about to come through the screen again, to get into this world.

"No!" Beatrice shouted from the floor of the stage.

I love you, Beets.

Then Isabelle launched herself at their twin enemies and knocked them backward. One of them latched onto her. She fought for a second and he pulled her through the screen. They were on the bridge over the chasm that joined the two worlds. A place between worlds. Between words.

BANG. The bridge began to collapse at the far end. *BANG. BANG. BANG.*

38

Isabelle fell.

At first she was spinning, tangled up with the two versions of Mr. Cecil. All three of them smashed into the already disintegrating bridge, which tipped to one side. The ropes snapped and they continued downward. Isabelle clutched at the air, looking fearful, then her face grew still and calm.

I love you, Beatrice.

Then she was gone, over the edge of the abyss and down. There was no sound. She just vanished into whatever lay below.

"Stop! Stop!" Raul shouted. He was running down the aisle, a fireman's axe in his hand.

Beatrice stood right at the edge of the screen. It flashed green. The image of the other world was like looking through a shattered pane of glass.

"She's gone," Beatrice said. "Gone."

The picture was flickering with grey and black, and the landscape had disappeared.

Raul said, "The projector is smashed, but the screen seems to have its own light source. We have to destroy it. Just in case they somehow use it again."

"She'll never come back if we do," Beatrice said. "She may still be alive down there."

"So could they. She wants us to keep them down there."

Beatrice nodded. Deep in her heart, in that place she shared only with her sister, it didn't feel as though Isabelle had gone. She had never before considered what it would be like if her sister died. Had imagined them old and travelling together. Isabelle's fans would have long moved on and she'd have Izzy all to herself. Just the slightest glimmering of light between them.

Raul ran out of the room and came back with cans of paint and varnish. "These were in the projector room." He splashed the solvent across the screen. Some of it went through to the other side in a few places, but portions hung between the two worlds.

He raised a pack of matches.

Beatrice took them but hesitated.

"We have to," he said.

"I know. Let me do it."

She held the wooden matchstick so tightly it nearly broke. Then she struck it, watched the flame, caught a whiff of sulphur, and threw the match. The solvent burst into orange flames that ran along the screen, burning it quickly, the smoke rising to the ceiling. They watched the flames grow, and then they descended the steps and backed up the aisle as the fire got hungrier, eating the fabric, the other world becoming ashes. Then the heat was too much. The flames leapt onto the curtains and across the banisters and they both decided to run. Beatrice stole one final backward glance to see that the screen was mostly gone, fluttering down in pieces of ash. Behind it was only a wall of stone.

Oh, Isabelle. Poor, brave Isabelle.

They raced out to the truck, the flames following them as far as the door. There was a loud explosion inside the theatre. She knew the fire brigade would soon be there.

Raul was able to easily start the truck. They backed off the sidewalk and went up the road. It was a long trip, and they took several wrong turns, but the sun was rising as they approached La Casa Grande. Under the light of a rising sun it seemed old and rundown.

The guards were gone from the gate. She and Raul pulled up to the front door and parked.

"Do you want me to go in with you?" Raul asked.

"Yes. Yes. Please."

It was early and the servants were already preparing breakfast as if nothing had happened. Though Mrs. Madge did not appear. The smell of bacon made Beatrice salivate. She went to her uncle and aunt's room. Betty was still sleeping in the bed. Beatrice felt no need to wake her.

She walked to the India room. Uncle Wayne was sitting in a chair in his bathrobe, his pajamas on underneath. His eyes were wide with surprise.

"He's gone," Beatrice said.

"Did you . . . ? Is he dead?"

"I believe so. As dead as he can get."

"And you killed him."

She shook her head. "Isabelle did."

"And where is she?"

She faced our enemy. She was stronger than all of us. All of these things crossed her mind. "I don't know. Gone. Maybe forever."

He let out a sigh. "Some father I am."

Beatrice nodded.

"I hope you can be happy someday," he said. "I never will be again."

"I don't know that I'll ever be happy. Not without Isabelle. But we stopped something truly horrible from happening. Someday I might find comfort in that."

Uncle Wayne said nothing, instead turned his head and stared out the window.

Beatrice and Raul walked through the French doors and out into the garden. They didn't stop until they were near his cottage.

"Thank you, Raul. I know . . . I know what will happen next." She pointed around her. "All of this falls apart without Mr. Cecil. But whatever happens we'll always be close."

"Yes, we will," he said. He placed his palm against her cheek. "You were very brave."

"And so were you. An artist with a hammer."

He didn't even smile at that. "I know sometimes you feel—I don't know the right word—ugly. But you're not. You don't look the same as your sister. You look different. That's all. A unique beauty."

She placed her hand against his. "Thank you. And Isabelle was even more different and beautiful than I understood."

He nodded. "I must see my father. Anything could've happened while we were gone. It was such a horrible night."

"Yes, it was."

She hugged him and felt his heart beating next to hers. Then she let him go.

She went back up to her room, her sanctuary, the place she and Isabelle had shared for nearly thirteen years. Her sister's clothes were still in the closet.

"Oh, Isabelle," she said. Then, finally, she sobbed.

EPILOGUE

1927–1939

Aunt Betty and Uncle Wayne continued their wardship of Beatrice until she was sixteen.

The mansion was soon lost to back taxes. Beatrice said goodbye to Raul and his father and promised to write.

"I expect to see more of your drawings," she said. "Every day, if possible."

"I'll send you as many as I can," he said. "I might even sign a few of them." Then he and his father got into the truck and drove off.

Uncle Wayne rented a small apartment near the HOLLYWOODLAND sign and played bit parts in a few movies to make ends meet. But sound films were soon the only ones being made and his voice was too ragged for audiences to enjoy. He became a bartender. Aunt Betty found employment, and perhaps some joy, sewing costumes.

Isabelle remained a mystery to the papers and magazines, the silent screaming girl who had vanished. Many assumed she had died in the fire at the theatre along with Mr. Cecil, who had also disappeared. Beatrice decided that Isabelle would have liked that story. It was dramatic, at least.

In time the people who'd watched Isabelle on the screen, who had loved her and wished to be her parents, her brother, her sister, her protectors, forgot that she'd existed. Many of the silent film stars retired as the "talkies" took over. *Frankenstein* was never released. The only copy had burned up in the Theatre Eternal.

When she was sixteen Beatrice packed up her suitcase and returned to the farm outside Lethbridge. She had a small log house built there. She finished her schooling, took more schooling, and received an anthropology degree. She travelled the country by train, then the world by ship and airship and airplane, and spent many years just seeing what there was to be seen. Her favourite place was the pyramids at Giza. She visited them twice.

She kept journals, and those journals eventually became books that people in many countries read. She often received letters from young women who said she'd inspired them to travel. On their own. To see the world. To own it with their eyes and minds.

But no matter how much she wrote or how far she travelled she only felt half of herself.

Then she returned to the farm, to the log house she had built, and became a teacher. She was known as Miss Scarves to her students, because she continued to wear scarves over her head. They were from every land she'd set foot in.

When she had been back at the farm for several years, she received a letter from Raul. It had several small drawings in it. One was of her scarves: *I seem to be able to make a living from these chicken scratches. I often think of you, friendbird.* It was addressed from Mexico City. She had never seen the ancient ruins there.

I will go one day, she decided.

When *The Wizard of Oz* came to Lethbridge, she decided to take the long drive into the city. She had never had the courage to enter another movie theatre again, but this time, this time she would go in. After all, it was the book she'd read to Isabelle at least ten thousand times. Beatrice steeled herself as she sat in the theatre and waited for the projector to show her that other world.

It was in the black-and-white scenes at the beginning and the end of the movie that she first spotted something. Just a movement out of the corner of her eye. A figure. It set her heart racing. She stayed for the second showing and watched that exact place on the screen and was certain she had seen something amazing. At the late-evening showing it became perfectly clear.

Isabelle was there. She was far in the background of the movie and was waving. Beatrice looked around the crowd. No one else seemed to notice her sister. But she was there, smiling and waving. And Beatrice felt that the place inside her heart, the place that belonged only to her and her sister, was full. Isabelle wasn't dead, perhaps would never be dead. Beatrice came back for the showing the following day and later watched *Babes in Arms* and there was Isabelle again, a character walking in the background. She winked at Beatrice. Actually winked!

Beatrice rented a hotel room across the street and watched ten more movies. She saw Isabelle again and again. Always the same age. In the background. Enjoying that other life.

A few days later Beatrice went back to the home quarter and into her house. She sat by her mother's stove, which had survived the fire. She'd had it cleaned and fixed, and she used it every day. Her mother had heated her father's coffee on this stove. Her father had heated their milk on it. In some ways her father and mother were still in the room.

It came to her, that night. Films were a view into another world. And somehow, Isabelle had survived in that world. Her spirit had become indomitable. The screen held so many stories. Her sister had fallen into one, then another, was perhaps going from story to story now. Just like people did in real life.

Beatrice smiled as she pushed another log of wood into the stove. Isabelle had won. They had won.

ACKNOWLEDGEMENTS

No book leaps fully formed from the void. I'd like to thank Hadley Dyer, Scott Treimel, Alice Kuipers, Kenneth Oppel, Chandra Wohleber, and Maria Golikova for helping to bring this book out of the darkness and into the light.